Deadly Surrender

Katie Reus

DEDICATION

For every reader who asked for Logan's story.

CHAPTER 1

Grace's heels clicked against the marble floor of the Serafina Casino and Hotel. A huge, glittering chandelier hung high above the lobby, the crystal reflecting prettily over the lush setting. The lights cast a soft glow, making the place feel almost magical. Likely smart staging so that people would want to come here to spend their time and money.

She would be doing exactly that, but she wouldn't be gambling. Tonight she was meeting up with a group of her friends and she'd dressed to the nines. As a guidance counselor, she normally wore comfy shoes, pants and cute tops. She was busy at school, and when working with kids, comfort was key.

In general, everything about her was "cute." She was never going to be voted most beautiful or be the kind of woman that men did double takes for. But tonight she actually felt kind of stunning. And after the year she'd had, she needed the ego boost.

Since this was Thanksgiving week she had the whole week off and she was taking complete advantage of it. Nights out with friends, a couple art classes, maybe she'd even catch a movie.

And if she was lucky she would get to spend time with her friend Logan MacNeil, who got her all sorts of hot and bothered. Of course they were just *friends*, and that wouldn't be changing anytime soon—or ever. But a girl could still fantasize.

Which she did. A lot.

"Grace?"

Her daydreams of what Logan might taste like turned to ice at the sound of a very familiar, very unwelcome male voice beside her. *Noooooooo.* This could not be happening. She'd left her past behind. Far, far behind and run all the way from California to Vegas to start over. So what the hell was *he* doing here? Maybe this was some weird waking nightmare?

Pasting on a fake-ass smile, she turned to her right to see Kevin, her ex-fiancé and also the man who had left her at the altar, standing there with his arm wrapped around his new wife, Sabrina. Pretty, blonde, tanned, toned Sabrina with the sculpted arms. She wasn't even the woman he'd been cheating on her with. No, she was someone new.

Grace wasn't sure how she kept her smile in place, but somehow she did. Looking her best tonight sure helped. Her dress was a sparkly, wild thing completely out of character for her, but it made her feel good. "Kevin? What are you doing here?" Okay, she could be civil-ish, but she wasn't going to say it was good to see him. Because she simply couldn't give that much of a bald-faced lie without choking on it.

"We're taking a vacation since it's Thanksgiving week. Figured we'd hit up the casinos and have a good time." God, had he always looked so freaking smarmy? Kevin was good-looking for sure, his dark hair always styled just so, and he was a runner so he was in good shape. But he was also obsessive about his looks, and as she stared up at him now, she realized...she did *not* miss him. She didn't miss feeling as if she'd never measure up to his bizarre standards, as if she was never put-together enough to please him.

Okay, then. She really didn't want to stand here having this conversation, especially when his gaze dipped to the V of her sparkly little dress. Seriously? He had the balls to check her out after what he'd done—and while he was standing there with his new wife? It was a dick move and now she was fantasizing about punching him in his balls. Or his throat.

"Well it's a fun city," she said neutrally. There, that was polite enough.

"Yeah, I thought I'd heard that you moved to Vegas. What are you doing here tonight?"

Before she could respond, Logan strode across the lobby looking good enough to eat in dark slacks, a button-down white shirt, and a black jacket that did nothing to hide his muscular form. Yep, there were the fantasies again. How many times had she dreamed about running her fingers over his broad shoulders as if she had every right? This was a man worth fantasizing about.

She shut that thought down as he approached and gave him a real smile. Even though she hated that he was going to meet her ex, she loved that he was here. Was relieved, even. "Logan!"

He approached the three of them, his eyes slightly narrowing on the couple as he wrapped a muscular arm around Grace's shoulders, pulling her close.

Grace was too stunned by the shockingly possessive display to step back, but why would she? She *liked* having his arm wrapped around her. She leaned into his hold, wrapping her arm around his waist. Oh yeah, she could easily give in to the fantasy now, pretend they were a couple. She'd imagined it often enough.

"I'm Logan," he said in a cool tone, holding out a hand for both of them.

Grace had a perverse sort of satisfaction when Sabrina's eyes widened slightly at the sight of him.

It wasn't like Grace could blame her. The man was walking, talking sex appeal. With reddish-brown hair, a killer Hollywood smile and adorable dimples, not to mention that edgy, lethal aura that just seemed to surround him, he drew female gazes wherever he went. Hell, male gazes as well. His body was pure, rock-hard perfection and she just knew he had to be incredible in bed.

"Kevin?" Logan said after they'd introduced themselves, a hard-to-read glint in his eyes.

Oh no... One night Grace had drunk just a teeny bit too much and told Logan about Kevin so he definitely recognized the name. She tensed slightly, embarrassed that Logan was meeting this loser at all.

"I owe you, man," Logan said, surprising Grace and apparently Kevin as well, because her ex-fiancé frowned even as Logan continued. "If you hadn't been such a dumbass, I never would have scooped up this gorgeous, smart woman and convinced her to marry me. See you guys later." Without waiting for a response, he practically dragged Grace in the direction of Cloud 9 restaurant. Or "the Cloud," as everyone who worked there called the place.

"I can't believe...you just did that," Grace whispered as they stepped into the noisy restaurant. Logan just waved the hostess away as he continued steering Grace, who was basically on autopilot right now as she digested what he'd just done.

"I saw your expression when you were talking to him. You looked like you were in pain."

Her gaze snapped up to his. Dang it, she thought she'd covered her disgust well. "Really?"

He shrugged, winking at her, his playful grin in place. And that grin? No sane woman could resist. Her panties had probably just combusted. "No. I just recognized that asshole's face."

She blinked, ignoring the rush of people and noise around them. "Wait, how do you even know what he looks like?"

Instead of responding, Logan shrugged again, giving her a smile with more than a hint of wicked in it. Good God, no wonder women threw themselves at this man. She wanted to count herself among them.

"Why did you do that?" she continued.

"I wanted him to think you were taken. And let's face it, I'm awesome. Of course he's going to be jealous now that he thinks you're with me." His voice was as teasing as his expression, though there was a glint of...something else she couldn't even begin to define.

She burst out laughing as they reached the bar where a few of their friends were already waiting. "You're ridiculous."

"True. But still awesome." His grip around her tightened as he continued maneuvering his way through the place, avoiding tables, people and waiters.

She loved that people just seemed to move out of the way for them when she was with him.

Her friend Taylor, who was married to Logan's twin Roman, jumped off a barstool and threw her arms around Grace. Grace was taller by a good four inches, so she leaned down and hugged Taylor back tight.

"What are you two laughing about?" Taylor asked.

"You wouldn't believe it, but my ex-fiancé was in the lobby and Logan told him we were engaged. You should have seen the look on Kevin's face as Logan dragged me away after thanking him for being a dumbass and letting me go." She laughed again, amusement filling her as she thought of Kevin's expression. She hadn't felt even a twinge of...anything when she'd seen him. Well, anything other than disgust and annoyance that he'd somehow encroached on what she thought of as her turf. Which she knew was ridiculous. Vegas was a huge city. Still, he should be banned forever. How was that for a fantasy? One where she never had to see her ex's stupid face again.

Taylor snickered. "That's crazy. And a very Logan thing to do."

"No kidding." She glanced over to see Logan ordering drinks, the female bartender giving him a wide smile as she took the order. Grace couldn't help but wish she was his for real. That there had been no acting tonight on his part.

Grace looked back at Taylor and realized she'd missed what her friend had just said. "What?"

"I'm glad you're off this week. We're going to take full advantage, starting with tonight!" She lifted her own glass of champagne even as Logan slid a glass into Grace's hand.

Surprising her, he kissed the top of her head and didn't move away, though he continued talking to his brother about something work related.

She couldn't help but notice how close he was standing beside her as he basically caged her in to the bar area. He was standing in the same protective stance as Roman had taken behind Taylor, and Logan smelled absolutely delicious. All male spice and sexiness and she wanted to turn her face right into him and simply inhale. Which she knew was crazy pants but she didn't care. He was this warm, wonderful presence.

Even if it meant nothing, Grace ate up his closeness right now. Heck, she could appreciate everything about the man—even if she could never have him.

CHAPTER 2

"Thank you again for earlier," Grace said, raising her voice above the music.

Logan leaned in a little more than he needed to, but he would use any excuse to get close to her. Even in the crowded club he could smell her subtle perfume. It had faint vanilla undertones, but there was something that was all Grace. Something addicting that went straight to his head—and his cock.

"No problem." He wouldn't mind being her fake fiancé for as long as she let him, though he wanted more than fake with her. He wanted everything.

"Are you going to tell me how you knew who he was?" she asked, looking up at him with pretty brown eyes he often lost himself in.

Yeah, he hadn't thought she would let that go. Instead of answering, he simply grinned and tugged her away from the round high-top where the rest of their friends were hanging out for the moment. A whole crew of them had come out tonight. Many of them were off work, including himself. He'd just gotten off a job, and since Grace was a guidance counselor, she had the week off too. Normally she pulled her long dark hair back, but tonight she'd left it down in soft waves he wanted to run his fingers through.

"You're really not going to answer?" Her grin was infectious, her dark eyes sparkling, and he wondered if she'd had one too many drinks. She didn't drink much as a rule and he didn't think she had been tonight. And he hoped that smile was all for him. All *because* of him.

Because he couldn't help but smile around her too. She was smart, sweet, fiercely independent and, okay, gorgeous. And someone he found himself fantasizing about every damn day. He'd woken up with his fist around his cock because of her more times than he wanted to think about. Ever since she'd walked into his orbit, he'd had one focus. Grace. The first time he'd met her, her bright smile had nearly knocked him on his ass. When he looked at her, he wanted to smile too. Hell, it was impossible not to.

"I've gotta have some secrets." He pulled her close as they reached the dance floor.

She was five foot seven and fit perfectly against his six foot two frame. Tonight she had on some sparkly, multicolored dress he'd never seen her in before but it hugged all her curves, dipping low in front and flaring out with every step she took. It definitely fit in with the Vegas club scene. Every time she moved, a rainbow of colors shimmered across her body. Normally she wore jeans and flowy tops, but this? Oh, he liked this so much.

"Fine, be that way." She mock pouted as she started swaying her hips to the music.

He wasn't a big dancer, mainly because he didn't have much rhythm—but no way was he letting her out on the dance floor without him. He was claiming her for everyone to see even though she clearly had no idea how he felt about her. And she was pretty much the only one who didn't realize how into her he was.

He understood though. She'd gotten burned so bad before she'd moved here, so he was simply biding his time until she was ready for him. And if she decided she never wanted to take a shot with him, well, at least they were friends. Though that was something he didn't want to think about. Because he would always want more, and he couldn't even pretend to himself that he was okay with that. So he shut the thought down hard.

When some guy started creeping up behind her and getting a little too close, he gave the man a look that immediately made him back off.

It made Grace laugh and dance even closer to him. Good God, the way she moved was pure erotic fantasy. And her laugh? He wanted to drown in that too. To just soak up everything that was her.

"Heads-up, your ex is here," he murmured as he leaned down closer. He didn't want to hurt her with the knowledge, but he wanted her aware that the loser had just stepped onto the dance floor. "Want to put on a show?"

Her eyes widened as she looked up at him. And he noticed that she didn't look around to see if he was telling the truth. No searching looks for that loser who'd left her on their wedding day. Maybe she didn't care about her ex anymore. She never talked about him. Maybe...she was ready to move on?

"What do you have in mind?" She raised her voice again, still moving in tune with the music.

He leaned down, making his intentions clear. Things were about to change between them, even if this was just for show. Because he knew once he got a real taste of her there was no going back.

Her eyes widened slightly but she didn't pull back. Instead she leaned into him, and when he slanted his mouth over hers, he hoped that this was more than just a show for her.

Because it was real to him. The taste of champagne on her lips made him go lightheaded as she leaned into him, holding on to his shoulders as she teased her tongue against his. He clutched onto her hips, savoring the feel of her curves pressed against him.

He hadn't had sex in forever, not since he'd met Grace. Hell, since before then. He'd been tired of the dating scene long before he met her. But he had a reputation and everybody assumed he was this giant player. He had been once upon a time, but that phase hadn't lasted long. He'd gotten tired of one-night stands and meaningless hookups but the reputation had stuck. Probably because he was a huge flirt.

He shoved thoughts of his past and everything else away as Grace plastered her body to his, wrapping her arms around his neck.

This didn't feel like a show; this felt totally real. So damn real he was afraid to hope for more.

And as he nibbled on her bottom lip, he realized he didn't want anyone else seeing them making out. Her kisses and moans and everything else were just for him. And the way she was melting against him completely caught him off guard. He'd just wanted a little taste. Now? God, she couldn't be acting. He sure as hell wasn't.

Holding her tight, he nibbled his way along her jaw, not bothering to hide his reaction to her. And she didn't seem to mind. "Want to get out of here?" he murmured before gently biting her earlobe.

She leaned her head back and looked into his eyes, her own wide with surprise and...heat. Undeniable heat. Her dark gaze searched his for a moment, but then she nodded, her eyes going heavy-lidded. "I just need to grab my purse."

This was it. He'd made his move and it was time to make her his.

CHapTer 3

Grace opened her eyes, stretching her arms above her head and bathing in the warm sunshine sliding across her naked body.

And froze.

She snapped her eyes open and looked around the exquisite hotel suite as last night came rushing back in naked, sexy images. Logan's head between her legs. Logan bringing her to orgasm over and over. Logan fisting her hair as he thrust into her from behind.

Ohhhhhhh. *Oh. My. God.* What had she been thinking? She hadn't been thinking, clearly. Or she wouldn't have indulged in a night of marathon sex with the man she'd fallen for ages ago. Why? Because he was *not* a commitment kind of guy. Not even close. He was in his mid-thirties and if he'd wanted to settle down, he easily could have by now. And she...she was a romantic who'd had her heart smashed to pieces nearly a year ago.

Cringing at herself, she swung her legs over the side of the empty bed. Her entire body felt not sore exactly, but she'd used muscles she hadn't in a while. And she was definitely tender between her legs. And okay, she also felt relaxed and better than she had in ages. Mind-blowing orgasms would do that to a girl.

As she stood up, she realized the shower was running and Logan was singing in an adorably off-key way. More images flooded back as she remembered making out with Logan in front of all their friends on the dance floor last night. *Oh*

God. Now everyone would know that they'd had a one-night stand. Which wasn't terrible but...with him, she wanted more. And some of her friends knew that. So now she'd have to deal with their well-meaning pity.

Embarrassment and a bit of panic surged through her. She scooped up her purse from the floor. She had another flash of Logan tossing it to the ground before he shoved her dress up to her waist—and dove between her legs like a man starving.

As her cheeks heated up, she started cataloging everything from last night in bright color images. Moving here had been a way for her to start over and put her painful past behind her. She'd made so many wonderful friends, and sleeping with someone who was part of their friend group was not part of her plan. It was just stupid. She didn't want drama or complications now. Or ever. But especially not now. Her life was getting back to normal and she felt...good most of the time.

And she could just imagine how nice Logan was going to be when he got out of the shower. Hell, he'd probably want to order breakfast and then have another round of sheet-burning sex before they went their separate ways.

Which...was just too much for her. She knew she was just another notch on his bedpost, or whatever that stupid phrase was. Logan was a giant flirt and hadn't had a serious relationship in pretty much ever, according to everyone. He didn't do them, apparently. She couldn't deal with a "this was fun, let's stay friends or hook up on occasion" type of conversation.

No, she was feeling far too raw after seeing her ex-fiancé last night and then... *This.* She found her dress draped across the couch in the little sitting room. Holy crap, what kind of suite were they staying in? Last night all her focus had been on Logan, and she'd been aware of the place he'd gotten but...this was incredible. It was all gleaming white and chrome and tons of natural light spilling in from the huge wall of windows.

How had he gotten such a great place so quickly? Oh God, was this where he brought his women?

Feeling nauseous, she grabbed her heels and slipped them on. Even though she knew this was Vegas, which had a very relaxed dress code no matter the time of day, she still felt vulnerable stepping out of the hotel room wearing such a skimpy, sparkly dress. Her walk of shame dress.

So she grabbed his aviator sunglasses and black suit jacket and slid them on. The jacket was big on her so she rolled up the sleeves. And she was grateful that it covered her dress.

Was she being a coward by running out without talking to him? Yep. She just didn't care.

The only thing she knew was that she had to get out of here now. She absolutely could not face Logan.

Nope. If she did, she might confess her stupid feelings for him and that was not happening. She'd already suffered enough hurt for one lifetime.

With her heart beating an erratic tattoo in her chest, she swung the front door open and realized they were definitely in one of the expensive suites, because this was one of the top floors of the Serafina. She was such a fool. Of course he brought women here. There was no way in hell he should have been able to secure such a great room on such short notice. Maybe it was one of the perks of working for the owner? *Bah*.

Feeling her cheeks heat up even more, she hurried down the hallway and pressed the elevator button, frantic to get away before Logan came looking for her.

Yeah, she definitely should've thought about things last night, like the repercussions of sleeping with someone in their friend group. Though to be fair, they hadn't done a lot of sleeping. God, she was best friends with his brother's wife.

But she'd been living in the moment. Seeing her ex had brought up all those feelings of insecurity and Logan had made her feel beautiful and wanted for the first time in forever. She'd been turned on and wanting nothing more than to finally have a taste of Logan.

Well now she'd gotten a taste and knew how incredible it was. Which just made this even harder.

It didn't take long to get to the parking garage, and she was so grateful she hadn't valeted her car the night before. There would be no waiting. Just running.

She felt a teeny bit bad about that, but embarrassment was riding her hard right now. As she pulled out onto the main road, she used her Bluetooth to call Sierra. Normally she would have called Taylor but that felt too weird right now since Taylor was married to Roman.

"Hey girl, how are you feeling this morning?" There was laughter in Sierra's voice.

"Embarrassed." She was grateful for the sunglasses as she pulled out onto the bright Strip.

"Why on earth are you embarrassed?"

"Because I made out with Logan in front of everyone last night?" Wasn't that obvious?

"So what? I nailed my man last night too. Who cares? You're single and he's single. You had a crappy year—that being an understatement. It's about damn time you indulged in some fun. Which is exactly what I've been telling you for the last few months! It's beyond time that you got yours!"

A weird sense of relief slid through her. Intellectually she knew she hadn't done anything wrong and she felt stupid for beating herself up. But some things had been drilled into her since she was young and they were hard to overcome. "Really? You don't think I should feel embarrassed?"

"Oh my God, no! Why would you feel bad? I mean, I can only guess what you guys did when you left, so... Was it great?"

"Incredible." That was all she was going to say about that. She kept getting flashes of the night before in her mind. Hot, naked, sweaty flashes as he kissed her entire body. God, the sexy growling sounds he'd made? *Yes, please.*

"You're totally giving me details later."

"No way."

"Hey, I tell you everything."

"Exactly. You give me TMI all the time." She didn't bite back a laugh because it was true. Sierra was so dang happy with her husband Hayden, and she told everyone.

"Whatever. So how was this morning? Was he weird?"

"I wouldn't know."

"Wait...why wouldn't you know?" Sierra asked cautiously.

Grace bit her bottom lip. "Well, I might have snuck out of the hotel room."

To her surprise Sierra let out a burst of laughter. "You're adorable and ridiculous. Man, your loser ex really did a number on you."

"True enough." No reason to deny it. "I just couldn't stand the thought of having that weird or awkward conversation with Logan where he told me last night was awesome and that he wanted to stay friends. Ugh, I'm such a coward. I cannot believe I ran out like that." She paused. "I also stole his jacket and sunglasses."

Sierra laughed even harder now. "You've got to stop! You're killing me. Just call him and talk to him. You'll feel so much better."

"I will." Soon enough.

"Good, because you know he's going to be at Friendsgiving tomorrow."

"Ah, crap," she muttered as she pulled up to a red light. She'd forgotten about that. A whole bunch of them were spending Thanksgiving together this year. And of course Logan was going to be there. "I'll call him, I promise." Yeah she definitely needed to call and apologize for running out of there like a lunatic. So what if they were going to have an awkward conversation? She should have just dealt with that in the moment and talked it out with him.

Gah. She internally berated herself as she took a left turn toward her neighborhood. It was too late to change things now.

The spicy scent of his cologne wrapped around her, and she realized it must be from his jacket. She liked wearing it, liked the sensation of it wrapped around her—and kinda wished he was currently wrapped around her instead.

Damn it, she needed to stop thinking about him, but that was pretty impossible when he was imprinted on every part of her now. At that thought her cheeks flamed hot, even though there was no one else in the vehicle with her.

After more teasing from Sierra, Grace ended the call, and by the time she got home she was feeling somewhat better. She needed to call Logan though.

She just...had to work up to it.

CHAPTER 4

Logan grabbed his phone and hit his second speed dial. "Come on, come on," he muttered. Water still dripped from his hair onto his bare chest as he waited for Grace to pick up. He'd come out of the shower moments ago and realized she was gone.

At first he thought she'd gone into the living room area maybe to call for room service. Then he realized her dress and shoes were gone. So was his jacket, for that matter.

"Hey," she answered on the fourth ring, her tone tentative.

"Is everything okay?" he asked, because he needed to know that first.

She shoved out a breath. "Yeah...I'm sorry for leaving."

Feeling as if he'd been punched, he sat on the edge of the bed, the sheets and comforter rumpled and half on the floor, half on the bed. "Why did you leave?" He simultaneously wanted and didn't want the answer. They'd had an incredible time last night. Of that he had no doubt. Maybe this morning she'd realized he wasn't what she wanted after all. He closed his eyes tight.

"I panicked and acted like a maniac?"

"Is that a question, or are you telling me?"

Her sigh was heavy. "I'm telling you. Look, I'm sorry. Last night was amazing but...ah..."

Oh no. He knew where this was going. She was going to let him down easy. Sonofabitch, he thought he'd played things right, that he'd waited until she was ready for more. Maybe she hadn't been ready for anything serious. "Please don't give me that speech."

"Well last night *was* amazing. So..." She cleared her throat.

"Yeah it was amazing. More than. And it shouldn't be a one-time thing." Hell no. He wanted it every night. And in the mornings too.

There was another long pause. "You've been such a great friend, Logan. I don't want to lose your friendship."

Sighing, he lay back on the bed, staring at the sparkling chandelier above him. The knots in his stomach tightened as he digested what she was telling him. Last night and then this morning had been incredible. He hadn't been able to keep his hands off her. She was even better than he'd imagined—and he'd had far too many fantasies. He'd made her come so many times and was desperate for more. To bind her to him so she never wanted to let him go. "I don't want to lose your friendship either."

"Okay good, then. So we're good?"

He closed his eyes. No, they weren't good. "Grace, I want—"

"I really value our friendship," she whispered, the raw vulnerability in her voice cutting at him.

Ah, hell. She'd said the word friendship about a billion times now. *Message received.* He wanted to push so badly but it clearly wasn't the time. Maybe it never would be. Maybe...she only saw him as a friend.

No, he needed to see her in person, to talk. "You're not going to lose that. I promise."

"I'll see you at Thanksgiving tomorrow, then?" Her tone sounded almost normal now. At least she wasn't whispering and sounding all sad and dejected. He couldn't handle that.

"Yes. Damn it, I mean no." He'd gotten a text from his boss, Wyatt, last night telling him he needed Logan for a job. Since he was the only single person on Wyatt's team who hadn't made Thanksgiving plans to travel out of town, he'd agreed. "I took a last-minute job thing. It shouldn't take too long but I definitely won't be there tomorrow."

"Well, I'll miss seeing you."

He was going to miss her too. "I'll text and send you inappropriate memes while I'm gone," he said to lighten the tension pulled taut between them.

She snorted, sounding much more like the Grace he knew and cared for in that moment. Not the Grace trying to have an uncomfortable conversation with him. "I look forward to your memes."

He could have teased her, could have said something about last night, but he got the feeling she was too raw. So he reined in the impulse to make a joke.

After they disconnected, he punched the pillow next to him, though it didn't make him feel any better. *What the hell?* He never should have gotten out of bed, never should have gotten in the shower.

If he hadn't, he would've been awake when she'd woken up and he could have gone down on her, convincing her that leaving was stupid. Hell, she never would have thought of leaving because he'd have been all over her.

As he sat up, he realized that his sunglasses were gone too. He shot off a quick text. *You steal my sunglasses too?*

She sent back an image of a fox swiping sunglasses, then followed with a picture of her wearing the aviators. Her dark hair was loose and a little rumpled around her face, and her smile was wide and inviting. And he wanted to reach through the damn screen and pull her close, kiss her senseless.

He'd wanted to finally make her his. Instead he'd ruined everything.

Laughing even around the pain in his chest, he responded. *Keep them. They look better on you anyway.* Then he saved her picture as his screen saver. Yep, he was a total masochist.

And now he felt like he was back at square one. Well, not square one, because now he knew exactly what she sounded like and looked like when she came.

He wasn't sure if that was better or worse. He just knew that he couldn't lose Grace.

Groaning, he shoved a pillow over his face.

CHAPTER 5

Grace sat back on the patio chair outside Sierra and Hayden's home. Thanksgiving aka Friendsgiving had been a success, and even though she hated that Logan was out of town and working, a very small part of her felt a thread of relief that she hadn't had to face him. Which made her feel like a big pile of crap. She really did hate that he had to work and be away from his friends and brother on Thanksgiving. But as part of billionaire Wyatt Christiansen's private security, both for the Serafina and the man himself, he was on call often and ended up jetting off to random destinations around the world. She groaned to herself.

"What's that groan for?" Taylor asked as she sat down next to her, a martini in hand.

Grace took a sip of her sparkling water. "Nothing. Just internally berating myself."

Taylor rolled her eyes. "What is it with you and feeling guilty over things you shouldn't feel guilty about? And don't answer that because it's not a question. You drive me crazy."

"I drive myself crazy." She always got so caught up in her head about things. It didn't matter that she was almost thirty, she still second-guessed herself as if she was back in college and unsure of her future.

"So what's going on with you and Logan?"

She went for what she hoped was a neutral expression and lifted a shoulder. "Nothing. Why?"

Taylor's bright blue eyes narrowed. "Really? That's all I get? I was so bummed that Logan had to work because I was looking forward to seeing the awkward interaction between the two of you." She lifted her glass to her lips.

"Hey! That's so messed up."

Taylor simply grinned. "I know. Roman and I have a messed-up sense of humor, what can I say?"

Grace snorted because it was true. Roman was so dry she couldn't tell if he was joking or being serious most of the time. "Look, we had fun, but we decided we just wanted to be friends." Thankfully he'd been texting her today and things seemed like normal between them.

Taylor gave her a strange look.

"What?"

"You both decided you wanted to *just* be friends?" Taylor asked hesitantly.

"Yes. Why are you being weird?" She took another sip of water, not liking being scrutinized.

"I'm just surprised, that's all." Again with the weird look.

"Whatever. I'm sure we have better things to talk about than Logan." Grace might not be able to stop thinking about him—and his very talented mouth and fingers—but she didn't want to obsess about him to her friends. *No, thank you.*

"Picture time!" Sierra said as she practically steamrolled everybody outside onto the patio. Hayden, Sierra's huge husband, was right behind her, and helping her shuffle people into place by the pool.

It was a miracle so many of their friends were there at the same time, though some of them had to work later in the evening.

Picture time saved her from having to talk more about Logan—at least for now, because her friends could be relentless. Still, she was trying to get grounded after the other night and wanted to focus on going back to the way things had been before.

Hours later after she'd finally gotten home, she found herself smiling when Logan texted her silly pictures of llamas and asked her how Thanksgiving had been.

For the next fifteen minutes they texted back and forth and she couldn't wipe what she knew must be a goofy grin off her face. Because apparently she really was messed up in the head.

She couldn't get enough of this man, even if she knew she was going to get her heart broken. Because after she'd experienced Logan in the bedroom? It was like he'd released something wild inside her that she'd been trying to keep locked up. Hell, something she wasn't sure had even existed before him.

When she was with him, all her insecurities seemed to fade away and she could be herself. It was incredibly freeing.

Now she wondered how the heck she was going to get over him.

CHAPTER 6

Logan scanned the surroundings of the quiet property and neighboring ranch as he slowly walked around the perimeter of the huge home. As far as jobs went, this one had been uneventful.

Though he hated being away from Grace and was bummed that he'd missed Thanksgiving with his friends, he'd been on much worse assignments when he'd been in the Marines and even while working for Wyatt. In comparison, this job was simple, and after being here a week, quiet. And quiet was *always* good for security.

Wyatt was working out some business logistics with Austin Brister, a wealthy rancher, and Brister had wanted to meet over the holidays to have everything ironed out by the time the new year rolled in.

Logan knew some of the details because he'd been on the periphery of a few of the actual meetings, but didn't really care about them. He was here to do a job—to make sure that Wyatt stayed safe. The man had made billions and was ruthless when it came to business. Fair, but still, a man with that much money had enemies. No surprise his boss had brought his wife Iris on this trip. And even though Iris was head of security at the Serafina, she still traveled with her husband whenever possible. In the last few years they'd become an incredible power couple in Vegas, both feared and respected. More than that, they plain loved each other. It was so damn clear every time they looked at one another.

Logan shoved his hands deeper in his thick down jacket as he rounded the corner of the house. They'd set up temporary electronic security in the vein of cameras around the property, but Wyatt was old-school and wanted a small crew patrolling physically, so Logan and a former Air Force pilot named Mia were outside in different areas right now. While Logan understood having feet on the ground, it was still cold.

Vegas got cold in the winter, but Montana was a different kind of icy and bitter. *No, thank you.* The ranch spread out for thousands of acres, but this man's house was fairly isolated and a solid twenty minutes from the nearest town.

He felt his phone buzz in his pocket but it was his personal phone so he didn't bother looking at it. Even though he wanted to see if it was a message from Grace, he rarely looked at or used his personal phone while he was on the clock. This job might be a cakewalk, but he never wanted to get complacent. Not when Wyatt's safety—which meant all of theirs as well—was on the line.

As he neared the back door of the huge ranch house, Julian, one of his coworkers, stepped out. In standard gear for a job on location like this, Julian had on dark cargo pants, a thick down jacket and a black beanie. "Too damn cold out here," he murmured, a half-smile on his face. At least a decade older than Logan, Julian would be retiring soon enough.

"How's it going in there?" They'd been in meetings all morning and Logan had opted to take the outside shift, even if it was cold. The fresh air made it easier to think, and right now his mind was on the future. One he wanted with Grace. If he could just figure her out.

"Good, I think. Nothing on the cameras and they're taking a break now. Brister has some calls to make or something. Why don't you head inside and grab a coffee?"

"You sure?"

Julian nodded and tugged his cap down. "Of course, man. You've been out here all damn morning. I'll take over the exterior for now. Then one of us can switch out with Benjamin." Who was currently manning the security feeds.

"All right. I've got my radio on me."

"I know. I'm good though. Take your time warming up."

Hell, maybe he would. The cold had gone bone-deep by now and the chance of anyone targeting Wyatt here was minimal. Logan pushed open the heavy wooden door and immediately savored the blast of warm air that met him.

He could already feel it seeping into him as he rolled his shoulders and shut the door behind him. Tugging off his gloves, he moved around the huge granite-top island toward the coffee pot. As he started to pour a mug, he froze.

"Stop!" A muffled female voice cried out from...somewhere.

He straightened, setting his mug down on the countertop. On quiet feet, he stepped out of the kitchen and headed in the direction he'd heard the voice. He knew the layout of the house—they'd all studied it before arrival as standard protocol. Wyatt had refused to meet with Brister until the rancher had sent over his architectural plans. Because yes, Wyatt was that paranoid, but he also had a hell of a lot of enemies.

Logan paused, waiting and listening. He knew he hadn't imagined the woman's voice but all was silent now. Everybody was supposed to be meeting on the opposite side of the huge house in an oversized living room with a roaring fire and a bank of windows overlooking a frozen pond. Brister's office was connected to it so no one had any business on this side of the house. And the man's wife had left to go grocery shopping a while ago, so she shouldn't even be here. But he'd been out by the barn and storage facility for a while so maybe he'd missed her coming back.

"You're hurting me."

The laundry room. Moving quickly and quietly, he hurried down the rest of the short hallway that led to a laundry room and four-car garage.

Pausing outside the door, he leaned in then quietly twisted the handle. Easing it open, he tensed, unsure what he would find.

As it swung fully open, he froze for only a second as Austin Brister swiftly punched his wife in the ribs.

Logan reacted on pure instinct and training. He didn't remember crossing the few steps of the laundry room, but suddenly he was in Brister's space, grabbing him by the shoulders and hauling him off his petite wife. The woman who'd only hours ago smiled so nicely at all of them and given them a quick tour before she'd left to buy food.

Rage popped hard inside him as Logan yanked Brister back and slung him across the room. Brister bounced off the front-loading washing machine.

"What the fuck are you doing!" Logan shouted even though it was pretty damn obvious the asshole was beating his wife. He had no tolerance for violence against women. Ever.

The man jumped to his feet, snarling like a raging bull. He was in his fifties, but strong and in good shape from ranching.

Logan somehow remained calm, though he kept his fighter's stance and Heidi Brister behind him. She reminded him of his own mother, but petite.

She had on loose jeans, a turtleneck and a cardigan with little Christmas elves on them. She was sniffling and crying quietly, and though he wanted to check on her, he needed to make sure the threat was neutralized. Because he knew if he turned his back on this guy, Brister would attack him from behind. No doubt. The kind of man who hit a woman—his own wife—would have no problem fighting dirty.

"Get the hell out of here," Brister ordered as he stepped forward menacingly. From the way he spoke, his swagger and tone, it was very damn clear he expected Logan to fall in line and follow his orders.

Which told him all he needed to know. This man wasn't going down without a fight. Still, he tried to keep a calm head.

Logan held up one hand as he pulled out his cell phone. "I'm not going anywhere. And if you take one more step, I will lay you flat on your back." He kept his voice as quiet as possible though it shook slightly from the pure, scorching lava of rage pumping through his veins. The way that man had just hauled off and nailed his wife like that.

He'd seen violence many times before. Too much of it. But this had stunned him, maybe because of the domestic setting. Hell if he knew, but he was barely holding on to his control, barely holding back from bashing this man's face in.

"This is all just a misunderstanding." Brister held his palms up as if he was surrendering. "I was just having a private conversation with my wife."

"Yes, it really looked like a conversation when you punched her in the ribs." Logan gritted his teeth as he held his phone up to his ear. "Julian—"

Brister rushed at him, moving like a bull.

Though Logan's instinct was to slide to the left and swivel so he could slam his elbow down on the man's back, he didn't want to give the guy any sort of opening to go after his wife again. Dropping his phone, he rushed straight at Brister.

They rammed into each other like two bulls.

Logan grunted under the impact of the other man's tackle even as he landed a punch to the gut. Brister hit back just as hard. Logan grunted against the pain of a shot to his ribs, but moving quickly and efficiently he decked the man across the face before slamming Brister onto his stomach. Wasting no time, he dug his knee into Brister's spine as he yanked the man's arms back.

"You're going to regret this," Brister snarled, struggling underneath Logan. "You're going to jail for assaulting me in my own home!"

Ignoring him, Logan secured the man's hands. On the job they always carried flex cuffs because they never knew when they would need them. He'd used them exactly twice before, and until two minutes ago he would have bet good money he wouldn't have needed them on this job.

"Ma'am, step around me and quickly exit the room," he said without looking over at Heidi. Sometime during the scuffle, she'd plastered herself against the washing machine, as if she was trying to make herself smaller.

God, Logan wanted to grab this guy's head and smash it against the tile floor. He could hear footsteps in the distance and quiet murmurs of alarm. Everything had happened so quickly but the backup team was on the way. Julian might not know what was going on, but he would have heard enough, thankfully.

Brister snarled at his wife. "Don't you go anywh—"

Logan gave in to the impulse and grabbed Brister by the back of the neck, cutting him off. "Unlike your wife, I punch back," he growled low in his throat even as Heidi hurried around him, her feet making soft shuffling sounds as she raced out.

Once she was out of the room, a sense of relief slid through Logan. No matter what shitstorm had just been unleashed, at least she was safe.

***

"You showed more restraint than I would have." There was more than a touch of savagery in Iris's tone.

Logan's mouth curved up ever so slightly. He wasn't sure *how* he'd showed so much restraint with that piece of garbage. The only thing Logan remembered thinking was that poor woman did not need to see even more violence. Because as far as he knew, this couple had been married for at least twenty-five years.

This definitely wasn't the first time that asshole had hit her. And Brister had gone for her ribs, somewhere no one would see. Logan gritted his teeth, thinking of the woman, about how she'd likely gotten used to the abuse.

"We're good to go," Wyatt said as he stepped back into the living room. He did a quick sweep of the room, his sharp blue eyes only softening once they landed on Iris. Unlike his normal suits, since he'd been here he'd been more casual in jeans, boots and flannel shirts. The look did nothing to take away from the authority of the man.

The police had already hauled Brister off even though he'd tried to claim it was a misunderstanding and that his wife would tell them "the truth." Logan had worried that since this was a small town and Brister was a very wealthy individual, they might look the other way. And maybe they would once Logan and the rest of them left. It made him feel ill.

He stood, unable to remain immobile anymore. "We can't just leave her here." Because no doubt the guy would be out on bail soon and then she'd be an easy target.

Wyatt's expression turned just as savage as his wife's tone had been. "We're not leaving her. She has a sister and brother-in-law she's going to go stay with. Her adult daughter lives close to them as well—and they're all across the country. I'm going to fly her on my plane. She's packing a bag as well as grabbing all of their financial records. I told her to take her time, to take anything she'll need when she divorces him. And I'll do a sweep of his records to make sure she gets everything she'll need. She's got a son who works in finance but he's in London, so trust me, she'll have the tools at her disposal to handle this."

Logan lifted an eyebrow. "She's leaving him for good?"

"Yes. She said her kids are out of the house. She said she's tired of being a punching bag. She was also adamant that he'd never hit the kids."

"Doesn't mean they didn't see or hear things," Iris murmured.

Yeah, no shit. Maybe there was a reason neither of his kids lived here anymore. Logan knew it was hard for women to leave their abusers, so he hoped this stuck. God, did he hope so. That man was a bull and she was so damn petite. Who the hell could live with themselves and actually hurt the one they loved on a continuous basis? "I don't think he'll make it easy on her."

Wyatt took his wife's hand in his, his smile a bit sharklike. "My attorney is going to represent her. She'll get everything she deserves."

Logan blinked, but he probably shouldn't be surprised. Wyatt was a tough bastard, but he had a soft heart where women were concerned. "Good."

"Well since it's clear this deal is not happening," Iris said dryly, looking away from the huge bay of windows, "are we going to head home after we drop Heidi off? I'm done with all this snow."

"Actually, I was hoping you wouldn't mind if we stopped over in New York. I have another meeting I should really do in person. I'd pushed it back, but..." Wyatt shrugged.

Iris lifted a shoulder. "Fine with me. The casino is a well-oiled machine at this point, and with Hayden and Vadim in charge I'm not worried about staying away."

Wyatt looked at Logan, eyebrows raised.

Surprised again, Logan shrugged. "I go wherever you say." Wyatt was the boss.

Wyatt gave him a hard look. "If you want to head home, we can trade out security. Mia's headed home, but Julian is coming. It's okay if you want to trade out with someone."

Logan shook his head. Even though he wanted to get home to Grace, he figured that some distance between them probably wasn't a bad thing right now. He'd obviously spooked her with that marathon of wild sex—and wasn't that a hit to his ego.

No, he would give her the distance she needed. They'd been texting nonstop and he was trying like hell to keep things normal between them. He was pretty sure he was succeeding but he figured the distance would help them both.

Hell, he needed to keep his own head on straight if he was going to figure out how to approach her, how to fix what had happened between them. Because he couldn't lose her. She was too damn special, too damn *everything* for him.

CHAPTER 7

I'm back. Are you free?

Grace nearly jolted as the text from Logan came through. Was she free? Yes, she was.

And nervous about seeing him.

It had been four weeks since he'd been gone on business and she missed him like crazy. They'd texted every day, but everything had stayed fairly surface-level. Which was good, but she had a feeling that tension they were both trying to avoid was still lingering right below the surface. They'd had a ton of hot sex and hadn't talked about it. It had to come up eventually, right? Or maybe he was fine never talking about it.

She texted back. *Yep. School is officially out for two weeks and I just got home.*

Up for some company?

Oh...he meant right now. She was still wearing her pajamas she'd worn to school since the last day had been pajama day. *Feel free to stop by.*

I'll be there in five minutes.

Tension ratcheted up inside her. Five minutes wasn't any time at all to mentally prep. Which was probably a good thing. Less time for her to stress out. She didn't bother changing out of her school pajamas either. This was who she was and she wasn't going to run around trying to find something sexy to wear. Besides, they were friends anyway. *Just friends.*

Instead she started a pot of coffee because the man was always drinking the stuff no matter the time of day. Then she peered into her fridge.

Old takeout boxes that she definitely needed to throw away. Taking a chance, she called a local Chinese restaurant that delivered and ordered his and her favorites. Because yeah, she knew his favorites.

When the doorbell rang a few minutes later, she tried—and failed—to ignore that familiar rush of nerves she experienced every single time before she got to see him. Tugging open the door and seeing him for the first time in weeks sent another rush through her, but this one was pure, raw longing. How was it possible that he'd gotten even sexier in the last month?

"I've missed you," he said as she opened the door. In dark slacks, a plain white button-up shirt that did nothing to hide his hotness, and an open black jacket, he looked like his put-together self—and she wanted to jump him. Then that sexy mouth of his curved up into a wicked smile as he took in her attire. "And nice reindeer ears."

Oops. Laughing, she tugged them off. "It was pajama day at school." She pulled him into a tight hug, fighting off that awkwardness that threatened to pull her under—and simultaneously tried not to sniff him like a weirdo. It was hard though when he was all masculine and delicious and looked as if he'd just stepped out of a cologne ad. Still, she somehow curbed the urge to shove her face against his chest and inhale. Because friends did not go around smelling each other.

"I started a pot of coffee for you," she said as she stepped back, tugging him inside with her.

He shut and locked the door behind them. "You are a wonderful woman, Grace Foster."

Her cheeks flushed. Oh, the awkwardness was there, but she kept her expression normal. Or she tried to. She was not going to act all weird because they'd slept together. It had just been sex. Something she'd been telling herself for weeks. "This is very true. So how was all the traveling? It seems like you guys did a bit more than normal this time." Weeks more. Not that she'd been counting or anything.

"This trip got extended because the first deal fell through. I can't actually talk about it for legal reasons, but one trip led to another. I'm glad to finally be home and I'm not planning on going anywhere for a month. Wyatt's got me at the casino at least that long. I think he felt bad about all the travel."

That warm, fuzzy feeling inside her blossomed. Logan would be home for a whole month? Yeah, she really liked that. Waayyyyy too much. Still, she ignored all the tingling in her girly parts, because no way. They'd simply had a one-night thing composed of a whole lot of sex. But they could not repeat that. Her heart couldn't take the eventual ending of things between them. Besides, he hadn't brought anything up, and if he'd wanted to talk about it, they would have by now. And she'd convinced herself she didn't want to talk about it either. So...things were good. Normal.

"I also ordered Chinese food," she said as they stepped into her kitchen.

He, of course, went immediately for the coffee pot as he always did. "Is it because you have absolutely nothing in your fridge?"

"I have stuff in there." She paused. "All old takeout food."

He snorted as he lifted the mug to his lips. "You have the palate of a twelve-year-old."

She grinned because it was true. She'd never learned to cook well. And she didn't care.

"You should let me cook for you." He watched her over the rim of his mug.

Cooking for her? Oh, she definitely liked the sound of that. But they were veering into weird territory because friends didn't cook for each other. Did they? No, definitely not. "So did you just stop by because you were in the area?" she asked, ignoring his offer because she didn't know how to respond.

He'd actually made her soup once when she'd been sick, and she was ninety-nine percent sure he hadn't just bought canned soup and dumped it in a container. Because she'd heard his brother teasing him later about all the effort he'd gone to.

"I have sort of a favor to ask."

She straightened, surprised but really glad he didn't seem to want to talk about their one-night thing. "What is it?"

"My parents get into town tomorrow. They're going to be here over Christmas break and I love them. So much. But...I'm tired of them asking me when I'm going to settle down. Now that Roman has Taylor, he doesn't hear it anymore. And it's like they've doubled up on me."

"Uh, how can I help?" She wasn't sure where he was going with this.

"Be my fake girlfriend."

Her eyes widened. She...hadn't been expecting that. And she wasn't sure how to respond. She couldn't very well tell him no. Well she supposed she could, but after what he'd done when she'd run into her ex-fiancé, she would be a pretty crappy friend if she said no. And they hung out all the time anyway, so... "Okay, but is Roman going to narc you out?" Because that would be pretty embarrassing.

"No. It was his idea."

She laughed aloud at that, even as a bit of tension settled in her chest. Being his fake girlfriend had some pitfalls—because she wouldn't be pretending when it came to her feelings. "As long as your brother and Taylor are on board, then I'm in. Though I do feel kind of bad lying to your parents." She'd never met them but she just felt bad in general about lying.

"It will be fine, I promise. My parents are actually really awesome, I just can't deal with the hounding this year."

She hesitated, pushing down her real feelings and hoping the truth wouldn't bleed through. "Then I would be honored to be your fake girlfriend." She would like a whole lot more, but that certainly wasn't happening.

He'd started to respond when the doorbell rang.

"That would be our food." Thankful for the interruption, she went to grab her purse but he waved her off and headed for the front door.

She wanted to argue with him but had done this dance before. When he decided he was paying for something, that was that. Logan could be very stubborn.

Sexy and stubborn... *Nope, stop thinking like that.* Logan was her friend. Well, now he was her fake boyfriend.

Unfortunately now they were going to have to act like a real couple. It wasn't like they would get into a full-on make-out session in front of his parents but still, they would have to be affectionate with each other. Or at least hold hands or something. *Just great, Grace.*

But it was too late to back out now.

CHAPTER 8

Grace ignored the butterflies in her stomach as she pulled into Logan's driveway. She saw Roman's truck as well so he and Taylor were already there, thankfully. The four-door Honda CRV must be his parents'.

Wind kicked up as she slid out of the driver's seat and told those stupid butterflies to cut it out. Of course they didn't listen because she was about to see Logan.

Sighing at herself, she grabbed the bottle of red wine she'd brought along with her purse. As she made it to the front door, she didn't even get a chance to knock before it swung open.

She sucked in a quiet breath as she came face-to-face with her walking, talking fantasy.

Logan looked sexy and delicious as always. His reddish-brown hair was slightly tousled and he hadn't shaved in a couple days, giving him an even more rugged look. Oh sweet Lord, what was he trying to do to her? A rush of heat flooded through her as she smiled up at him. He was everything she wanted but couldn't have.

He pulled her past the doorstep and into his arms.

"Grace! I'm so happy you're here." He kissed her on the mouth, the kiss teasing, lingering, and still over far too quickly. Heat flooded between her legs this time as she remembered how he'd kissed her hard before taking her up against that hotel room wall.

What...was he doing? Why had he kissed her like that? It took her all of two seconds to realize that his parents were standing in the foyer as well, watching her with curious smiles. And she noticed that their suitcases were still there.

"My parents just arrived. Their flight was delayed," he said, his eyes sparkling.

Oh, that was why he'd kissed her. Of course. "Oh, if we need to move the dinner, then—"

"Absolutely not," the woman who was very clearly his mother said. The red-head who was at least five feet ten, slender and lean stepped forward and pulled Grace into a tight hug. "We're late but we're so excited to see our boys and I'm so happy to meet the woman Logan has been talking about."

Grace hugged her back even though she felt a little weird about lying about the whole situation. "It's nice to meet you guys as well." She held out her hand for his father but the dark-haired man pulled her into a bear hug too.

Okay then, they were definitely huggers, which made her laugh a little. She could see where Logan had gotten his good nature from, if his smiling parents were any indication. Already they were such a contrast to her own mother and she liked it.

Logan looped an arm around her shoulders and pulled her close, which she was thankful for. It might feel a little odd for him to be holding her like this, but it also felt...good. Soooooo good. Her lips were still tingling a bit from that kiss, making her feel lightheaded as it was.

Multiple voices grew louder for a moment, and Grace knew that was more than just Taylor and Roman in the kitchen. She looked up at Logan quizzically.

"Some of the guys from work are here too," Logan murmured.

"Look, we're going to put our suitcases upstairs and get settled in if that's all right. But we'll be back down here in a few minutes," his mom said.

Logan nodded. "Sounds good. And I'll grab the suitcases."

"Thanks, sweetheart." His mom patted his forearm gently. "And Grace, I just want to be clear that even though we're staying here, don't feel like you can't stay the night. We're all adults and I know you're important in my son's life."

Grace felt heat flood her face and could imagine how pink her cheeks were. But she wanted to mess with Logan just a little bit because of that toe-curling kiss and this entire situation he'd sprung on her, so... "Oh, I don't stay over here. I told Logan that until I have a ring on my finger, no sleepovers."

She kissed a shocked-looking Logan on the cheek as she hurried out of the foyer, wine bottle and purse in hand. As she made her exit she heard his mom say, "I think I like that girl."

She snickered to herself as she stepped into the kitchen and found a whole crew of guys from his work standing around plates of appetizers and going at them like rabid coyotes. Even though it would be weird acting like Logan's girlfriend in front of some of their friends, it would also make this whole situation easier if it was a big party and not just his parents and brother and sister-in-law.

Taylor threw her arms around her. "I'm so glad you're here! The freaking sausage fest right now is out of control. And they're acting like they've never seen food."

Behind her, Roman simply shook his head as he opened a bottle of beer, his mouth twitching ever so slightly.

"Let's head out to the patio so we can gossip," Taylor said, linking her arm through Grace's.

"Sounds like a plan to me." She set the bottle on the countertop and let Taylor guide her outside into the fresh night air.

Multiple palm trees were lit up with twinkle lights, their fronds waving prettily around the pool. Even though it was too cold to use the pool right now, she was glad it wasn't covered because of the way it glittered under the moonlight.

"So you and Logan are 'together'?" Taylor asked, using air quotes.

Rolling her eyes, she nodded. "Apparently. I couldn't say no to him when he pretended the same thing for me with my ex, and then looked at me with those puppy dog eyes." The dismissive words hid her true feelings. Or Grace hoped they did.

"He's a sneaky one."

She frowned at her friend. "How so?"

Instead of answering Taylor just snorted. Then her eyes lit up when her husband stepped outside with two glasses of wine in his hand. Roman, the perfect gentleman, handed both of them glasses. "I'm going to hang out here with you guys for a little bit. I'm about to lose a hand in there."

"Too much sausage for you?" Taylor giggled before taking a big sip of her wine.

Grace grinned at her friend. "How much have you had to drink?"

"I've only had two glasses. Well, now will be three—but I didn't eat lunch today." She giggled again at nothing in particular, making Grace smile.

"So are you happy to have your parents in town?" she asked Roman.

"Yeah, we don't get to see them enough. They keep talking about moving here, and if you and Logan tie the knot, maybe they will." As usual, Roman's expression was dry. Seriously, how were he and Logan twins?

She snorted. "Don't you start on that too. I know you know the truth—" She cleared her throat as Logan stepped outside with his parents in tow.

They'd shed their jackets and each had a glass of something in hand as Logan made a beeline for Grace.

His beautiful eyes narrowed ever so slightly as he once again wrapped his arm around her shoulders. "I'm going to get you back for that parting shot," he murmured in her ear before gently nipping the lobe.

She couldn't think of any sort of witty response because she felt that nip all the way to her core. Because suddenly she had a flash of that night in the hotel room. Him behind her, thrusting hard, wrapping his fingers gently around her throat as he leaned forward and bit down on her earlobe, whispering dirty things. Making her come.

That man and his wicked, wicked mouth.

Blinking, she realized she needed to keep her shit together because his mom was now looking at her and asking her about working in the school system.

"It's great," Grace answered. "I'm definitely going to enjoy my Christmas break, but I love what I do. The kids are all fantastic. Whenever I hear people talking about 'kids today' and how awful they are, I wonder if they actually know any children because they're simply wonderful. And they make me feel hope for the future." And the kids she worked with were in high school and so ready to get out there and change the world.

"Yep, I knew I liked you." His mother beamed at her.

Another dose of guilt wormed its way inside her. This woman was so nice and Grace didn't like pretending to be something she wasn't.

"Tell my mom about the new program you implemented," Logan said.

She was so used to deflecting talking about herself or simply listening to others—a huge part of her job as a counselor—that it felt weird to be almost bragging about herself.

But when Logan looked down at her with clear admiration, she brushed aside her stupid insecurities. Logan always made her feel important, as if she had something valuable to contribute and say.

Just another reason she wished this arrangement was real instead of a charade.

CHAPTER 9

Grace steered her car into Logan's driveway, smiling to see him already outside with all of his Christmas lights. It looked like a tangled mess. She was actually surprised he'd decided to put up lights so close to Christmas at all, and she had a feeling it had more to do with his parents being in town than anything else.

Before she'd gotten out of the driver's seat, he was right there in well-worn jeans, a long-sleeved T-shirt shoved up to his elbows and a sexy grin that competed with the roped forearms he was showing off.

"Hey." She handed him one of the coffees she'd picked up on the way here. A breakfast blend with a hint of sugar—his favorite.

"Hey yourself." He kissed the top of her head and she wished it had been her mouth instead. "I'm surprised you showed up."

She narrowed her gaze. "Why? I said I'd be here." Last night as she'd been leaving, he'd asked if she wanted to come over and help put up Christmas lights. She'd assumed it was for part of the show with his parents.

"I know. It's just early and I know it's your break. I thought you'd sleep in a bit." He glanced back as she popped the trunk. "What's in there?"

"You'll see." She grabbed her purple and blue vinyl foldout chair in its carrying bag with her free hand—which he immediately took from her even though it weighed maybe four pounds.

"What's this for?"

"I plan on watching you hang up all the lights while I enjoy my coffee." She was kidding. Mostly.

He laughed in that full, deep way she felt all the way to her bones as he shut the trunk. "So by helping, you actually meant supervising?"

"You know it. If I'm going to be part of this farce, I figure I need to act realistically. This is my Christmas break and I'm not planning on doing any extra work. This is Grace in holiday mode." She took a sip of her coffee. "Besides, I already put up all my stuff a month ago. You're kind of a slacker."

His grin was gorgeous, revealing one of his dimples. "Fair enough." She followed him across the lawn where he set up her chair in seconds. "Now you have a perfect view of me and my sexy ass."

She simply rolled her eyes but sat in the chair, crossed her legs and sipped her perfectly doctored coffee, watching him expectantly. "Well? You better get that sexy ass in gear. Those lights aren't going to hang themselves." Oh, she shouldn't flirt but she couldn't help it. This had been them "before" the sex. Before the hotel room. Before all the orgasms that had clearly rattled her brain.

That wicked smile never faltered as he picked up a bundle of white lights. "So you *do* think my ass is sexy?"

"I'm not going to answer that. Your ego is already big enough. I don't need to stroke it any more." He opened his mouth and she could tell he was going to say something about the word stroke. So she held up a finger, grinning. "Leave it."

He snickered and turned around, actually shaking said ass as he headed toward one of the bushes lining the front of his house. Oh God, she'd missed this flirty, fun banter they'd always had. And she wished... Ugh, it didn't matter what she wished. She lived in the real world.

If Logan wanted a relationship, he would have made it clear. And she wasn't sure he was capable of one anyway. Capable of giving her what she needed.

At this point in her life, Grace wanted the whole package. Marriage, a real family, maybe kids. But she wanted a committed man who came home to her and had eyes for no one else. Maybe she was broken or something. Maybe she wasn't going to get all that. Maybe...she needed to stop being a Debbie Downer and get her head out of her ass.

"So where are your parents?" she asked, needing conversation so she'd stop getting caught up in her thoughts.

"Out to breakfast with Roman and Taylor. They said it was pathetic that I'd waited so long to put these up and weren't going to help me either. By the way, my mom really likes you," he tossed over his shoulder as he started stretching out the lights on the grass.

Once she finished her coffee, she actually was going to help him. She just needed this boost of caffeine before she got going. "I really like her too. Your dad as well, though he's pretty quiet."

"Yeah, he usually lets her do all the talking," Logan said laughingly. "I didn't really think about my plan because now she wants to know when you and I are getting married. She told me I needed to put a ring on your finger immediately." He didn't look at her as he spoke, focused on pulling a knot out of one of the strands.

"Is that right?" That weird sensation settled in her belly at the thought of wearing Logan's ring but she shut that down fast and tight. She'd worn someone's ring before—a beautiful, sparkly one—and had gotten burned. It didn't matter that on her wedding day she'd been having a panic attack *before* she'd found out the groom wasn't showing up. Right before the ceremony she'd worried she was making a huge mistake, and then it hadn't mattered because her ex had made the decision for her.

"Yep. I definitely didn't think this whole thing through. I thought it would get her off my back. But now that she's met you, she said no one else will ever compare so I might as well do the right thing."

Grace forced out a laugh at his words, glad it didn't sound strained, and set her coffee down. "Well, I'm pretty awesome, so I don't blame her." Striding across the lawn, she picked up the other end of the string of lights and tugged them away from him. "You're making an even bigger mess. And why don't you have a light storage reel so you keep your lights tangle free? This whole scene is just sad."

"'Because I'm not organized' seems like the obvious answer," he said dryly. "Do you actually organize your lights?"

"Of course I do. Light storage reels are a thing. It's a big wheel that's awesome. I keep my decorations in bins and I keep my lights tangle free when I put them away. Makes it much easier each year to put things up."

He just grinned at her and stood back as she started untangling.

She shook her head. "No way. You're not going to stand there and supervise while I do all the work. Hold this end up while I work on this tangle."

"You're sexy when you're bossy."

She felt her cheeks flush but she ignored the sexy comment because at this point that was all she could do. Maybe it was her imagination but she felt like there was this simmering, underlying electric current between them. It was different than the banter they'd had "before." And she knew exactly why. Because they'd seen each other naked and been intimate. That changed everything.

Suddenly he stiffened, his gaze going past her shoulder.

Grace started to turn but he grabbed her arm. "Run!" he shouted as he yanked her toward the garage.

It was instinct to try and look at what was going on, but every fiber of her being trusted him. Dropping the lights, she ran as a sudden firework of pops rang out.

Her legs were moving of their own accord as the rat-a-tat grew louder and louder, dirt and grass flying up all around them.

Belatedly she realized this was... Gunfire? *Oh my God!*

Logan threw his body over hers as they barreled into the garage, his vehicle and hers in the driveway giving them cover as they slammed against the hard concrete.

Just as quickly as the storm of gunfire arrived, it disappeared.

"Grace!" She opened her eyes to find Logan staring down at her, running his hands over her arms and chest and down her body worriedly. The way he was looking at her made her realize he must've said her name more than once.

"Are you okay?" she rasped out. Her heart was stuck in her throat.

"I'm fine. Are you hit?" He ran his hands down her legs now.

Blinking, she pushed up from the concrete floor and looked around in a daze, her heart a wild thump in her chest. "Was that a drive-by shooting? And are you sure you're okay?" She knew she'd already asked, but she swept her gaze over him, looking for any signs of injury. She couldn't believe what had just happened, was trying to wrap her mind around it even as she tried to steady her erratic breathing.

He nodded as he pulled her to her feet. "Come on," he ordered, guiding her inside his house, already pulling his phone out—to call the police, she assumed.

What the hell had just happened?

CHAPTER 10

Grace felt as if she was on autopilot as Logan gently helped her stand from the metal-backed chair in the detective's office. She didn't actually need the help but right about now she wasn't afraid to admit that the drive-by shooting had shifted her whole world. Even hours later she felt as if her insides were still trembling.

She hadn't seen anything, hadn't seen the shooter, hadn't even seen the vehicle. Nothing. But she'd heard the gunfire and had run like hell. Now the sound of the shooting was embedded in her brain and was all she could focus on. As bullets slammed into her car—which had been towed to an auto shop by now.

"Thank you for making your statement," said Detective Hurley, a tall man with wide shoulders. His dark hair was cropped short and his equally dark eyes were kind, making her feel more at ease. He stood from across his desk and met them on the other side.

She simply nodded because of course they'd made a statement. They'd had no choice. Someone had tried to kill them. Logan had actually gotten a make and model of the vehicle which surprised the heck out of her because everything was a fuzzy memory of noise and fear.

The gunshots. Running. Being tackled to the ground.

It had all sort of happened in a tunnel, as if it had happened to someone else and not her. And it had been so fast. That was the thing that blew her mind. How quickly the violence had come, then gone, as if it had never been there at all. One of Logan's neighbors had gotten a partial of the license plate because he'd been outside with his dog, which felt like a miracle to her.

"You've got my number if you remember anything more," the man said to Logan, who just nodded and murmured his thanks again.

"I feel like there's more we should do," Grace said as they stepped out into the hall. She knew there was realistically nothing they could actually do at this point, but whoever had shot at them was still out there. And that scared her. Especially since they had no idea if it was personal against one of them or random violence.

Logan wrapped his arm around her shoulders and she instinctively leaned into him. "There's nothing we can do. We're just going to let the police do their job." He said the words, but for some reason she didn't quite believe that he was going to do *nothing* about this. He worked in private security for a very wealthy man. A man with a sort of ruthless reputation. "I'm going with you to your place," Logan added in a tone that indicated he thought she might argue.

"Okay." Grace did *not* want to be alone right now. She didn't even have a car, would have to call her insurance company and figure things out later.

"It's going to be okay," he said quietly.

She leaned into him for a moment as they reached the end of the hallway and stepped into a crowded, slightly loud open area with a lot of desks and uniformed officers. "I know. Or I hope so. You're handling all of this very well." He seemed so okay with everything and she felt as if she might split apart at the seams.

"It's not the first time I've been shot at." His tone was neutral. "And I'm not handling the fact that you were there very well at all." Now his jaw tightened and she saw the first spark of raw anger in his eyes since they'd gotten here.

"Well I'm pretty pissed that you were shot at too. I know what you told the detective, but do you think this has anything to do with your job?"

He shrugged as they made their way through the cluster of desks. "It's too hard to know. I work security for a wealthy man, so he's the one who's usually the target, not me. But yeah, I could have made an enemy. Only one name pops to mind though, and like I told Detective Hurley, that man is currently sporting an ankle monitor and is under supervision."

She nodded because she'd heard everything Logan had told the detective. Some guy from one of Logan's last jobs had been beating his wife and had been arrested after Logan's interruption. He'd only been let out on bail because he was rich, and they'd put an ankle monitor on him to make sure he didn't leave the state and go after his wife. Grace knew enough about domestic cases that the fact they'd actually put an ankle monitor on him surprised her, so she wondered if someone had pulled some strings to make that happen. Or maybe the judge had used common sense and realized that a man with that much wealth would be a risk to go after his wife and finish the job. And of course the Las Vegas PD would be checking to make sure the guy was still where he was supposed to be.

In a way it made her feel worse, because if their attacker wasn't that guy Brister, then Logan had no other suspects. Which meant some random person had just taken shots at them.

As they stepped outside, she jerked in surprise to find Logan's parents, and Roman and Taylor all waiting on the sidewalk. She hadn't realized Logan had even called them.

Before she could move, Taylor pulled her into a tight hug immediately. Feeling her best friend's arms around her soothed some of her frayed edges.

"How are you holding up?" Taylor asked as she stepped back, her bright blue eyes filled with worry.

"I'm okay. We're okay." Maybe if she said it enough, she would start to feel it more. She just wanted to go home and curl up in front of the fire and block out the rest of the world. And she was really glad that Logan was coming with her. She definitely didn't want to be alone right now and he was such a strong presence. Even with her own inner turmoil, she felt safe around him. Always had.

To her surprise Roman pulled her into a big hug too, lifting her off the ground. Then he moved on to Logan, hugging his twin tight. "I packed a bag for you," Roman said. "Already put it in your truck. And Mom and Dad are staying with me so you don't need to worry about anything else."

"Thank you," Logan said quietly to his brother before looking at Grace, his expression neutral.

She wished she knew what he was thinking, but ever since the shooting it was like he'd gone into a sort of lockdown mode. She'd never seen him like this and it was throwing her off-kilter even more. It wasn't like she expected him to be his fun, joking self, but he was in what she assumed must be his operator mode for jobs. It was a different side to him and she was grateful to have him with her.

After getting hugs from his parents and saying a quick goodbye, they were on their way in his truck, which hadn't sustained any real damage thankfully. She felt bad that he was leaving his parents right now around the holidays when they were in town specifically to see him and his brother, but she couldn't dredge up too much guilt. Being shot at was a damn good reason to go home and hide out for the night as she tried to reset her brain.

"I understand if you want space when you get home. I'm not leaving, but I'll give you space once we're there." Logan's voice was low, soothing, as if he was afraid she'd break down.

Surprised, she turned to look at him. "I don't want to be alone tonight." And it wasn't like he could go back to his place anyway. Sure, he could go to his brother's, but she wanted him with her.

He shoved out a breath. "Good. If this happened because of me, then I'm sorry—"

"Logan, even if this has something to do with one of your jobs, it's not your fault. Whoever shot at us? They're at fault, and I hope like hell they get caught sooner than later."

"Me too." Reaching out with one hand, he linked his fingers through hers.

She didn't think to stop him, just squeezed him back tightly as she laid her head against the headrest. Right now she could use some comfort.

And even though he seemed to be handling this so well, she figured he could use comfort too. Someone had tried to kill them right outside his home in broad daylight.

If the cops didn't catch whoever had been behind it soon... She didn't even want to think about what that meant.

CHapTer 11

"Come here," Logan murmured to Grace. Standing in the middle of her kitchen, she looked lost and out of sorts and he wanted to do everything possible to comfort her.

Thankfully she didn't pause, just stepped forward and wrapped her arms around him as he did the same to her. They'd just gotten back to her place and she definitely wasn't her normal self—which was understandable.

"It'll get better," he murmured.

He knew her mind was in a state of shock as it tried to reset itself to this new reality in which someone had just tried to kill them on a bright, seemingly calm day in a quiet neighborhood where she should have been safe. Safe was a relative concept, but Grace had never been to war, had never even fired a weapon, as far as he knew. Her world was not violence.

She kept her face buried against his chest, and even though the circumstances were less than ideal he still liked holding her. Liked having her soft body pressed up against his so trustingly.

"Is there anyone in your family you want to call? Maybe talk to them about what happened?" He would be there for her, but he didn't want her to bottle anything up.

In response she made a snorting sound and simply shook her head. When her grip around him loosened, he finally released her, letting go of her soft, warm curves.

"You don't even want to call your mom?" he asked.

Sighing, she sat at the center island and rubbed her hands over her face before looking at him. "No. Because it would eventually devolve into a conversation about her. Trust me."

He started rummaging around in her pantry, looking for hot cocoa because he knew she liked it. "You don't talk about her much." And he was more than curious about her relationship with her family.

"We really only talk a couple times a year. She has a very good job out in DC. She was transferred there about five years ago and hasn't left."

"So why don't you guys communicate much? I mean, only if you want to talk about it," he added. He wanted to keep her talking right now but only if the conversation wouldn't make things worse. She just been through a shock, a trauma really, and he wanted to help her get back to normal. He smiled when he found the box of hot cocoa packets.

"It's not really one thing. She wasn't a terrible mother, I guess. But she wasn't a great one either. Her love was very conditional—it always came with strings. Her whole life she was looking for someone to fill a hole inside her and I was more or less an inconvenience. She was all loving and wonderful when she didn't have a boyfriend. And when I was young, I loved those times. It was always the two of us and she loved doing stuff together. But the second she got a boyfriend, I basically ceased to exist. Around the time I hit twelve, I realized it had nothing to do with me and I stopped trying so hard to win her love back. The only reason I even recognized it is because my grandmother spelled it out for me, in words I would understand, that I wasn't doing anything wrong."

"Jesus, Grace." He'd never known. Never guessed it was anything like that. He knew her dad wasn't in the picture because he'd split town before she'd been born.

She simply shrugged but he saw the flash of pain in her dark eyes as she continued. "If her current boyfriend had younger kids, which they often did, I became their babysitter. Which was fine for a while. But they filtered in and out of our lives so often that I hated getting attached to anyone because I always had to say goodbye. So I stopped trying to please her and she definitely noticed that."

His heart ached for the little girl she'd been, who'd had a mother who couldn't see how incredible she was. "I'm sorry."

She lifted a shoulder. "She is who she is and she's not responsible for my happiness. I accepted it and accepted that I'm definitely not going to get the positive relationship from her that I would have loved to have at one point. I tried well into college to keep a relationship going with her, but I'm done trying to fix something that can never be fixed... Something that never should have been broken in the first place." Her words were so matter-of-fact.

He put her mug in the microwave and pressed start. "Is that why you got a degree in psychology?"

She grinned at him and he felt that smile like a sucker punch. "You're very astute. I didn't even realize it at the time but that's exactly why I went into psychology. And then I discovered that I wanted to work with kids, and here I am." Her smile faded a little bit but some of the edge of her tension seemed to have eased up.

Pulling the mug from the microwave, he stirred it a bit before passing it over to her. "How do you feel about watching a movie before you crash?" In the military he'd found that watching movies, being able to let his brain relax, had helped hugely after dealing with a shock of violence. That and exercise to the point he was beyond exhausted. Different things worked for different people.

"Thanks for this." She blew on it gently. "And yes, mainly because I don't want to close my eyes. Is that pathetic?"

"I think it's pretty damn normal." And she was an even more incredible woman than he'd already thought. "Do you want me to pop some popcorn?"

She grinned. "Sure. I'll go pick out a movie. Superhero movies only."

"I think I can live with that." Yep, the circumstances were definitely less than ideal but he still loved being with Grace. And he was going to be her shadow until they figured out what was going on. He would never let anything happen to her. Not on his watch.

He wanted to push her a little on what kind of future they might have but knew tonight wasn't right for that. She needed to feel safe, to have no pressure. But that didn't mean he'd given up on making her his. After seeing her with his family last night he'd realized even more how real he wanted this fake relationship to be.

CHAPTER 12

Grace stepped into her kitchen, surprised to find Logan there—shirtless—cooking breakfast for her. This was definitely a fantasy come to life, but she'd tossed and turned all night and was too tired to fully appreciate it.

Yawning, she headed straight for the coffee maker. "You made pancakes?"

"I'm a man of many talents," he said, more than a hint of wicked in his tone.

She couldn't even snort out a laugh because yes, he was. During the movie last night, she'd started dozing so he'd gotten her up to her bed and she'd crashed hard—alone, unfortunately. But it hadn't been a great sleep. She'd thought about asking him to stay with her, but had held back, not wanting to do something they would regret. "You certainly have a healthy ego." She inhaled the rich scent of her French roast. Perfection.

"It's called confidence, baby," he said as he flipped a pancake.

Baby? She kinda liked that, but she ignored the little flutter in her belly. "If those pancakes are as good as they look, then I'll go with confidence instead of ego."

He laughed, the deep rumble coming out of him absolutely delicious. Good God, everything about him was delicious. "So...any news?" She pulled out her creamer and started doctoring her coffee.

"Nothing from the police. But some of the guys from work installed some new cameras around my property. In the front and backyard."

Frowning, she sat at her center island. "You already have cameras." She'd seen them. Considering he was in security it made sense he had them. Heck, a lot of her neighbors did too, to make sure no one stole their deliveries.

"Yeah, just directly around the house. But these new ones are an extra precaution. They put them up in areas where they're hidden. I'm going to stay away from my place and see if anyone comes back. At this point, it's possible it was just a random gang initiation thing, but I still want to be smart."

She shuddered slightly. She was glad he wasn't going back there anytime soon even though she hated the entire situation. "You can stay with me," she blurted out. He could easily stay with his brother or even at the Serafina. She had a feeling his boss or someone there would comp a room for a while.

"Thank you. I was hoping you'd say that."

She blinked. "Really?"

"I don't like that you were with me when it happened. I can't imagine that you were the target, but still, I want to be with you, to keep you safe." There was a protective note in his tone.

Warmth settled inside her, spreading outward in a soothing, all-consuming wave. "Well thank you. I hope my guest bed was okay."

He slid another pancake onto a growing stack of them, then opened a carton of blueberries. "I could always stay in your bed," he said, tossing a grin at her over his shoulder.

That was the Logan she knew. Sweet, teasing, flirty. As much as she liked the idea of him staying in her bed... "That's not a good idea and you know it."

"I don't know any such thing. The last time we were in bed together we both enjoyed it." His voice dropped again, with a completely different tone.

Oh, she wasn't touching that with a ten-foot pole. She was feeling far too weak where he was concerned. And the casual way he talked about their time together only drove home the point that it had meant more to her than him. "So what's on our agenda for today? I know you said you wanted to meet up with your parents. Is that still on?"

He paused. "I'm going to let you drop the subject of sleeping arrangements for now, but we're going to revisit them again."

She simply buried her face in her coffee as he continued. Noooo, they would not be revisiting anything.

"And to answer your question, Taylor wants to go to a skating rink today, of all things. I've never been but apparently she loves it so we're all meeting up there, including my parents."

"That actually sounds like a lot of fun." And it was so close to Christmas.

"Better bring your A game. Taylor and Roman are competitive, so we're going to have to skate circles around them."

She laughed. "Well I hate to disappoint you but I'm not competitive about ice skating. In fact, I think the last time I skated I was maybe fourteen. You're going to be sorely disappointed if you think we're going to skate laps around anyone."

"That's okay, you can just hold on tight to me." His voice dropped an octave, that hint of wicked back in his tone and his expression. "I'm a good enough skater for the both of us."

"Yep, confidence. You have far too much of it."

"Can you blame me? When Roman and I were born, I got all the awesome. Clearly." He slid a blueberry pancake onto a separate plate and her mouth practically watered at the sight of it.

"If that pancake is for me, then absolutely, we'll go with confidence."

"And?"

"And you got all the awesome."

He simply grinned at her and pulled out a can of whipped cream from the fridge. As he squirted a little dollop on it, she flashed back on a memory of the night in that hotel suite. She had no idea where the whipped cream that night had even come from. But the one thing she remembered oh so clearly was him squirting it down the length of her naked body before he licked it up.

She wondered if him bringing out a can of it now was intentional. Feeling her cheeks heat up as she remembered how he'd so easily brought her to orgasm that night—so, so many of them—she avoided his gaze as she stood to grab the syrup. Right about now she was going to drown herself in calories and sugar and completely avoid thinking about the raw, hot sex she'd been fantasizing about for the last four weeks. It was more than just sex, however. It was that Logan was everything she wanted in a partner.

When she looked over at him, thankfully his back was to her again as he continued to clean off the stove.

She just hoped she could get through today. It was getting harder and harder to keep her heart guarded. And who was she kidding? She'd fallen for him.

First she got left at the altar and now she'd fallen for one of her best friends—a sexy, sweet player who was never going to settle down.

Super smart, Grace. Suuuper smart.

CHAPTER 13

Grace felt like she was one second away from falling over as she slowly made her way toward the ice rink in her rented skates. Logan and Roman's parents were already on the ice and might as well be pros compared to her. Taylor skated by and did a spin, clearly showing off before winking at Grace.

She spotted Logan through the crowd of people skating around, his green skullcap a beacon. He'd wanted to wait for her, but she'd insisted he head out there and get some good skating in before she attached herself to him.

Her skates slipped as she neared the entrance to the ice. She was definitely in over her head. At least there were some kids out here who seemed to have no idea what they were doing. So she wouldn't be the only one who couldn't skate. Probably the only one over the age of twenty though.

As she stepped out onto the rink, her legs wobbled but at least she didn't fall. *Score one.*

"Glad you finally made it," Logan said as he zoomed in next to her, executing a perfect stop. He had on a zip-up hoodie that matched his dark eyes and his ever-present wicked grin firmly in place.

"We'll see how long I last."

He gently took her arm as she stepped out farther onto the ice. Her legs still trembled, but he held her steady and she liked the closeness. She swayed once, but thankfully managed to stay on her feet. Okay, she could do this. It might have been a while but maybe it was like riding a bike.

"You weren't kidding," he said, laughing as she took a few tentative steps forward, getting her bearings.

She narrowed her eyes at him. "Or maybe I'm just lulling you all into a false sense of security before I show off and start doing triple axels."

He lifted an eyebrow.

"Okay, I'm kidding. I'm pretty terrible. I might end up sitting out and drinking hot cocoa. Which actually sounds kind of amazing." She wouldn't have to worry about breaking any bones and she'd get chocolate. Win-win.

"At least do a few laps with me." He took her hand in his, and though she'd seen him loop around the place a few times with an impressive grace while she was still getting her skates on, he adjusted his pace to her snail-like one with ease.

"You really can go ahead." He shouldn't have to get stuck babysitting her.

He snorted. "What kind of boyfriend would I be if I left my girlfriend stranded while I went off and skated all day? Hell, what kind of *friend* would I be?"

Her heart stuttered for a moment at the word boyfriend, even though she knew it was all part of the role he was playing. "Okay, point made. So have you heard anything from your friends at work about the shooting?" He hadn't seemed concerned about them coming here today, though he had been mindful about the route they took, taking an extra-long one to make sure they weren't followed. Which made her feel good and bad because there was potentially still a threat out there. But she knew he would never put her or his family in danger. She just kept hoping he'd gotten word that the person or persons had been arrested.

"Nothing concrete. Still digging." He lifted a shoulder. "They'll get a lead. They've got bullets and a partial license plate." Leaning closer, he was looking as if he might kiss her when Roman suddenly skated by.

"Come on!" Roman was skating backward, looking just a bit smug and like a big kid. She'd never seen Logan's more serious twin looking so relaxed.

Grace nearly jumped when Taylor hooked her arm through hers.

"I'll race you," Roman said to Logan.

Logan started to shake his head but Grace smiled. "Go ahead. I've got Taylor with me and you'll probably lap us." He hesitated, but she waved him off. "You better not let me go," she said to Taylor.

"Never. I thought maybe you were exaggerating about being a terrible skater." Taylor snickered as a group of ten-year-olds flew past them.

"Hey," Grace said, nudging her.

Taylor just laughed. "I'm kidding. You're definitely not that bad. I thought you might have to use those ice walkers that all the kids use."

"I looked into it and they were too short for me." Plus they'd all been taken by kids.

Taylor stared for a moment then burst out laughing as a cluster of teenagers smoothly skated past them.

"I'm not kidding." Grace wished she was.

"I know, that's why I'm laughing."

She started to feel more at ease as she stretched her legs, taking longer and longer strides, though she knew Taylor was basically moving in slow motion for her. She'd tried to keep track of Logan and Roman, but they'd disappeared into the crowd of people and she wasn't going to risk turning around and seeing when they would be coming up behind them.

"It feels kind of weird to be pretending to be his girlfriend," she said quietly when she was sure his parents weren't anywhere nearby. She'd seen his mom with her bright red cap skate by not too long ago.

Taylor raised her eyebrows. "I'm pretty sure Logan isn't pretending."

Grace frowned. "Whatever. We had a good time the other night but that's it." She wasn't going to put more into what happened than was there. That was a recipe for heartbreak. Of all people, she knew what it was to give her heart to someone and then have it crushed. She'd also experienced that with her mom early on.

"Okay. Just saying, I don't think he's pretending." She gave Grace a meaningful look.

It made no sense, but Taylor appeared to be serious. "What? Look, he's a total player. I adore him and have a great time with him, but...he's not looking for a relationship." And Grace had gotten burned so damn badly she was afraid to risk her heart again anyway. Because then she would lose Logan as a friend too, and the thought of that? Ugh. No. He was such an important part of her life.

Taylor started to respond, then both men skated past them in a blur. Logan pivoted, skating backward and very clearly showing off right before he tripped and fell on his butt.

A group of teenage girls giggled as they skated by and two younger kids on ice walkers easily moved around him.

Grace laughed only when she realized he was definitely okay. "Go on without me. I've got him," she said to Taylor. She slowly skated toward Logan, the blades slicing over the scuffed-up ice. She was going so slow it wasn't hard to stop herself. Before she could attempt to help him up, he popped to his feet with incredible ease, considering how slick the ice was.

"I won. Did you see me?" His grin was unrepentant.

Laughing, she took his outstretched hand. "I'm pretty sure everyone saw you. And they definitely all saw you fall."

He tugged her close as they skated over to the edge of the outer rink where it wasn't crowded. "You seem to be getting better at this." He kept his pace slow until they neared the side and stopped completely.

"It's a little easier than I remember, but I certainly won't be going backward or doing tricks." Or racing anyone.

Logan's gaze fell to her mouth and suddenly his expression was pure heat and hunger.

It took her off guard with its intensity. Heat blossomed inside her and she nearly jerked back in surprise when he leaned down and brushed his lips over hers. The kiss was far too fleeting, his lips grazing hers and leaving her burning up inside and wanting more as he pulled back. The place was completely inappropriate—she didn't want to get run over by skaters—but she still wanted more.

She stared at him in surprise, nearly losing her balance. But he took her arm and they pushed off again. "Were your parents watching?" she murmured, wondering at the show of affection.

"No. You looked adorable and I wanted to kiss you." He said it so matter-of-fact, as if of course that was why he'd done it.

Her cheeks heated up and she didn't know how to respond *at all*, so she looked away, focusing on the ice in front of her and not falling. It was difficult when she felt as if he'd imprinted her with that simple kiss. They'd done a whole lot more than that a month ago, but that kiss had felt...so intimate. As if there had been a shift in their relationship. Or maybe that was just her wanting more. She'd let Taylor's words get stuck in her head.

"Nothing to say to that?" He slid his fingers through hers, holding tight. Even with her thin mittens on she felt the warmth of him and wanted a whole lot more.

"You're maddening," she muttered. What was he getting at right now? They'd decided to be friends, so why did he want to go and mess it up?

"I get that a lot."

She snorted. "Oh, I bet."

He laughed in that carefree way of his she absolutely loved. Even though she got to spend time with him, this whole charade was starting to make her ache for more.

***

"Well I'm glad my son finally asked you out. And I'm glad we finally got to meet you," Logan's mom said as she slid into the seat across the booth from Grace.

She smiled, her fingers wrapped around her warm cup of cocoa. "Me too," she said, mainly because she wasn't sure what else to say. She'd given the rink a few laps but now she was done and was enjoying watching all the other skaters while she got her chocolate fix and fun eighties music blasted from the speakers. The rink had a few booths set up where non-skaters could relax and stock up on the fried food and hot cocoa.

"He's been talking about you, so I figured it was just a matter of time before he finally asked you out."

Wait...what? "I didn't know he'd talked about me." Her gaze strayed over to the rink where Logan, Roman and their father were acting like twelve-year-olds. Taylor was really no better. But Logan was definitely the ringleader of the group, doing spins and challenging everyone to do better. The sight made her smile, especially since Roman never acted this goofy. Logan just seemed to bring out the best in everyone, in her opinion. She included herself in that as well.

"Oh, yes. 'Grace is so smart and accomplished.' 'Grace said the funniest thing the other day.'" His mom's smile was so open and welcoming, and everything about her was so at odds with Grace's own mother, right down to the silly Christmas sweater she had on. "He thinks quite a lot of you."

Grace felt her cheeks flush. "I think a lot of him too." He'd been in the Marines, though he rarely talked about it, and he was one of the bravest, sweetest people she knew. But she didn't want to talk about her and Logan, since there really wasn't a *them*. "Logan tells me you guys are talking about moving to Vegas."

A smile spread across the other woman's face. "Yes. It seems as if both our boys will be staying put, and we're both retired now. Since we want to be closer to them, it's a very real possibility."

"That's great. I know they'll be happy to have you close."

"Are you two gossiping about me?" Logan appeared out of nowhere, sliding in the booth next to her.

The butterflies were back after that. Not that they'd ever really left.

"Of course not. We can find more important things to talk about than you silly boys," his mom answered, grinning as her husband collapsed next to her.

"Our boys are killing me," his dad muttered, a grin on his face. His mom just patted his arm and told him to sit tight while she grabbed him some hot cocoa.

Grace found herself wishing more and more that this whole thing was real, that she and Logan would be spending tonight together in her bed. That she'd get a replay of a month ago that led to something lasting.

That they had a real future of more than just friendship.

CHAPTER 14

"Today was fun," Logan said as he and Grace stepped into her kitchen. The familiar scent of her home, like warm vanilla, wrapped around him. He liked returning home with her, even with the threat hanging in the air. This whole situation was oddly domesticated, but he loved the thought of coming home to her every day. Or her coming home to him—of them sharing a place together.

She made a noncommittal sound as she disarmed the security system. She'd pulled her hair into a ponytail and her expression was carefully neutral.

Since they'd left the skating rink, she'd been unusually quiet. Under normal circumstances he didn't mind quiet, and sometimes craved it. But this was different. She was almost withdrawn. "Is everything okay?"

"Yes." She set her purse on the countertop and leaned against the white quartz. "And today was great. Sorry, I'm just caught up in my head, I guess. I know school is out, but I have a work day tomorrow—all the staff does—and I'm just wondering if I should even go in. I mean, it's not like the police think that drive-by was targeted, but I'm just getting up in my own head and letting fear take over."

He wanted to pull her into his arms but her body language screamed at him to stay exactly where he was. He might not like it, but he respected her personal space. "Is that the only thing bothering you?" Because she'd talked to his mom for a while and he wondered if his mother had said anything to upset her. Not intentionally of course, but still.

"Yeah."

For some reason he didn't believe her, but his phone buzzed in his pocket. When he saw it was Detective Hurley, he pulled it out. "It's the detective."

She straightened slightly as he answered and put it on speaker. "Logan here. And Grace is with me too. You're on speaker."

"Good, glad you're together. Sorry to bother you on a Sunday, but I wanted to give you an update. We found the SUV used in the drive-by. It was reported stolen a week ago by an older woman, and there have been multiple reports of random drive-by attacks in neighborhoods nearby to yours. Mainly malicious destruction. Mailboxes knocked over with baseball bats. We think we know who's behind it—some asshole teenagers, one of them related to the woman who reported her vehicle stolen. I just wanted to give you a heads-up on where we're at."

Under normal circumstances the man wouldn't be calling Logan, but the detective knew Logan's boss fairly well, so this was likely a courtesy call. "Thanks, detective. I've still got cameras up at my place so if anything out of the ordinary happens, I'll let you know."

"Thanks. You guys know to be aware of your surroundings and careful, but this whole thing is shaping up to be different than we originally thought. You'll probably see a news report about it tonight."

They spoke for a few more moments, and when they disconnected the tension in Grace's shoulders had eased somewhat.

"Well that's good news," he murmured, tucking his phone away.

She nodded, wrapping her arms around herself. He hated the distance between them, desperately wanted to comfort her. "Some people are such jerks. They're lucky no one got hurt."

"I hope they catch them before someone actually does." Logan thought of the potential loss of life, the complete pointlessness of something like this and how much worse it could have been. "At least it looks like we weren't targeted."

"Yeah. So...I guess you're going to head home soon, huh?"

Yeah, unfortunately. He liked staying at her place way too much. But he wasn't leaving until they'd actually talked about their future. Not just danced around it.

"Look...I keep telling myself the timing is crap, but now that it seems we're in the clear...I want to take you out on a date." He was done playing it slow. They'd been flirting and dancing around the tension between them and he was just done.

She dropped her arms, her dark eyes widening.

He lifted an eyebrow. "Are you really that surprised?"

"Yes?"

"Is that a question, or...?"

Her lips curved up. "Sorry, yes, you did surprise me. I didn't expect you to ask that."

"Why not?" He was attracted to her, he was more into her than he'd ever been into anyone, and he knew she was attracted to him... Why wouldn't he ask her out?

"I thought we'd decided to be friends," she murmured, her gaze skittering around the kitchen.

"*You* decided that. Not me. I had time to think while I was away for work. And I don't know what's going on or if I pushed you too soon after what happened with your ex, but I want to lay it all out there. I want to take you out. I like being your friend, but I want more."

"I don't know if we would be a good fit." She played with the hem of her sweater nervously, but at least she was looking at him now. He didn't like the insecurity he saw on her face.

"We fit pretty good weeks ago." He didn't need to spell out just how good they had. To his delight, her cheeks turned pink. He loved making her blush, loved saying dirty things to get her riled up. Just loved everything about her.

"That's not what I meant."

"Then what did you mean?"

"I just meant... You're not known for your dating skills."

He frowned at her, taking a step closer. "Are you calling me a player? I'm not sure if that's where you're going."

"Kind of. No, yes. Maybe." She lifted a shoulder.

He stepped even closer so that they were both leaning against the same countertop. "It's been a long damn time since I actually dated anyone. And yeah, I have a reputation, but I earned it ages ago. And for the record, I haven't dated anyone since I met you."

She frowned at him and he couldn't get a read on her.

"One date. That's all I'm asking for." Okay, that was a big lie—he wanted a whole lot more. But he didn't want to spook her. If she hadn't been so skittish and run out on him after that amazing night together, he'd be laying it all out there for her. "That night we shared was amazing and I value your friendship. But I still want to explore this thing between us." He reached out and tucked a stray lock of hair behind her ear before gently cupping her cheek. "It's pretty clear there's something special between us."

"I know," she whispered. "I'm just afraid of..."

"Afraid of what?"

She shook her head and it was clear she wasn't going to answer him.

"Say yes to the date. Give us a chance, Grace." *God, please say yes.*

"Yes. And it better be a good one," she added, her tone all sass.

He loved it when she got like that. He'd much rather have his feisty Grace than the nervous, insecure one.

"Good. What time does your workday end tomorrow?" Now that she'd said yes, he wasn't waiting to lock down a time and day. The sooner the better.

"It's basically just us cleaning out our offices and classrooms tomorrow. So, two o'clock maybe."

"Okay, I'll be here at five."

Her lips kicked up in amusement. "That's kind of early, unless you're a senior citizen."

"I didn't say I was bringing you home early, just that I was picking you up early. I want a full evening with you." He wanted as many waking hours as possible with this incredible woman.

There went that blush again, and God help him, he gave in to his impulse and leaned down, covering her mouth with his.

She leaned into him, curving her whole body up against his and holding on so damn tight and kissing him back so hard that a raw wave of hunger punched through him. She was all nerves and doubt a minute ago so this caught him off guard. But he was going with it.

Moving on instinct, he pinned her up against the countertop, rolling his hips against hers as their tongues teased against each other. He knew that if he pressed, he could have her naked again and take her right up on the countertop. And the floor. Then her bed.

But he didn't want a quick fuck. He wanted so much more from her. Even though it killed him to be patient, it was clear she needed it.

Her fingers linked together behind his neck and she sighed, molding against him as if they'd been made for each other.

Though it took everything inside him, he pulled his head back and tried to slow the wild beat of his heart.

She stared up at him, dazed, her fingers clutching his shirt.

He cleared his throat. "I'm taking you on a date before this goes any further. Besides, I don't see a ring on my finger," he murmured, drawing a startled burst of laughter from her. God, he loved that sound.

"True enough." Her mouth curved up into a sweet smile. "I can't believe I said that to your mom."

"It was hilarious. I think that's why she likes you so much." That and the fact that his mom knew how much Grace meant to him.

"Where are you taking me tomorrow?"

"It'll be a surprise." One he was pretty sure she'd enjoy.

"I think I can deal with that. Just don't expect to get lucky." Her grin was wide and a little mischievous.

"I would never expect. But I will be hopeful. Especially..." He leaned down and nibbled on her earlobe for just a moment. "Because I know exactly how you sound when you come." And he wanted a repeat. Many, many repeats.

She shuddered against him but then slid sideways and ducked out from under his arm. "You definitely need to sleep in the guest room tonight."

He groaned, his head falling back. She was right. "Are you sure? Seriously, if you don't want to be alone tonight—"

Shaking her head, she grinned. "I'm sure."

Damn. He knew it was for the best, but he wanted to be in her bed now.

Wanted forever there.

CHAPTER 15

"I hate to say this, but I think this is a seasonal place. I'm pretty sure they're closed." Grace squashed the twinge of disappointment as Logan pulled into the parking lot of one of those arcade/game places. She'd thought he would have put more thought into their first date and checked if it was open.

"Just trust me."

"Okay." She'd dressed in jeans and a pullover sweater since he'd told her to be comfortable and casual tonight.

He was dressed similarly in a hoodie and jeans that accentuated his perfect butt. She liked seeing the different sides of him. There was the sexy, buttoned-up Logan when he was in his suit for work, and then there was this fun-loving casual man. Though technically he was always fun-loving. And she loved that he brought out a relaxed side of her. More often than not she found herself laughing at something silly he'd said and all the tension from her day eased.

Before she'd even shut her door, Logan had rounded the truck and shut it for her, then took her hand in his.

"Is holding hands a first-date thing?" She shot him a sideways glance as they started across the empty parking lot. Little flutters danced in her belly at the simple act of holding hands, but she wanted to know what it meant to him.

"No. But we've been friends for a long time so I'm skipping a couple steps." He pinned her with a heated stare she felt all the way to her core.

Oh, how she felt it. "Sounds good to me," she rasped out. She was trying to be smart about this, trying not to get her heart completely broken, but it was so damn hard to put up walls between them. Because she couldn't *not* be herself with him and he was always himself with her, which she absolutely loved. Still, she was letting herself get caught up in her head, wondering if she was making a mistake. Shoving those thoughts aside for now because she simply wanted to enjoy herself tonight, she let him lead her toward the double glass doors.

Before they'd reached them, a man who looked as if he was in his mid-twenties unlocked the door and stepped out wearing rainbow-colored sneakers, a Henley shirt and ripped jeans.

"Logan, my man," he said, stepping forward and doing that fist bump/hug thing that guys seemed to do with such ease.

"Thanks for doing this," Logan said as he stepped back and slung an arm around Grace's shoulders. "Rick, this is Grace. Grace, Rick. He's opening the place tonight for just us."

"Oh, that's really nice, thanks."

"It's great to meet you. And any friend of Logan's is a friend of mine." Rick stuck out his hand and shook hers firmly, an easy smile in place. "I would do anything for this guy. He saved my brother's ass overseas and I will forever be grateful my big bro made it home."

Logan shook his head and cleared his throat, quickly brushing off the other man's praise. Grace was going to ask him more about that later but Rick waved them inside and kept talking.

"You guys are set for the night. Here are the unlimited game cards. They work for anything," he said, handing two of them to Logan. "I've got some paperwork and catching up to do in my office, but the arcade is yours as well as the go-karts for the next few hours. And as long as you *promise* to be careful, you can use the rock-climbing wall. Just don't hurt yourselves or I'm going to be in a shitload of trouble with insurance, since this is after-hours."

"Deal. We'll be careful. And thanks again." Logan steered her toward the open arcade and the flashing neon lights of all the games as Rick locked the glass doors behind them. While it was brightly lit, the place wasn't noisy like it would've been if it had been packed with a bunch of teenagers, with music blasting over the speakers.

"This is kind of awesome," she murmured, looking up at him and grinning. "And...he's serious about the go-karts?" It was pretty cold out, and normally these places closed the outdoor activities in the winter months.

"Yep. Right now only the arcade and indoor rock-climbing wall are open until about six every day. But as you heard, he's doing me a favor. So what do you want to do first? Go-karts, rock-climbing, or arcade?"

"Pretty sure I'm going to kick your ass in Ms. Pac-Man. And then we're playing hoops." She looked around the huge open space, greedily taking in all the games. No lines, no waiting.

He let out a startled laugh. "I thought you said you weren't competitive."

"I'm not competitive in things I suck at. But with Ms. Pac-Man? Prepare to lose."

He laughed again, the sound so free and wonderful, and she wanted to soak it in. "Challenge accepted."

Half an hour later, after she'd destroyed him in Ms. Pac-Man, they'd ended up tied in basketball and now they were side by side in one of those shooting galleries where they were defending the world against rogue dinosaurs.

"You're actually pretty good at this," he muttered as he narrowly beat her for a second time.

"Actually? What's that supposed to mean?" She shifted the fake rifle and pulled the trigger, killing a dinosaur on screen.

He was definitely faster and more accurate, taking out triple the number of raging dinosaurs that she did. "I didn't think you'd ever held a weapon."

"I haven't. Not a real one anyway. But I do like to play laser tag because yes, I'm a giant nerd. And I spent a lot of weekends at a local arcade with my friends when I was growing up." Being here reminded her of all those good times. Her mom had been absent half the time, so whenever her mom ditched her for a new boyfriend, Grace had ended up spending a lot of time at a place called Tito's Playland. Her name had been on the hall of fame for a couple of the games, though she was sure it had long since been cleared out by new winners. Heck, who knew if the place was even open anymore.

"I remember you told me how much you loved going to the arcade. I just didn't know how good you'd be at *this* game." Logan's jaw tightened in focus as he took out another dinosaur. He was so damn sexy when he was in "operator" mode, as she now thought of it.

"Is that why you chose this place? Because of what I told you?"

He shrugged and pulled the trigger again.

That...was incredible. "All right, I think I'm out for this one," she said as the game started to reset. It touched her that Logan had brought her here because of something she'd told him months ago. Maybe...they *did* have a chance of something real. She was just so afraid to hope for more. Getting left on her wedding day, being stuck in that little room in the chapel and being told by her friends that her fiancé wasn't coming, having to face a whole chapel of people...it had seriously messed with her sense of worth.

"How does rock-climbing sound, then?" he asked as he started putting the guns back in the holsters.

"Amazing." And it did. She didn't want to think about the past now, didn't want to think about her ex. This was such a fun and thoughtful date. And no matter what happened in the long run, she simply loved spending time with Logan.

He clearly knew his way around the rock-climbing area because he geared her up before putting on his own, making sure her harnesses were secure.

"So do you bring a lot of dates here?" she blurted before she could censor herself. Immediately she winced. She didn't want to ruin tonight and couldn't believe she'd asked that. "Oh my God, I'm sorry. I don't know why I asked you that. The question popped into my head. Can we just forget I asked?" They were friends, so she was way more open with him than she'd ever been with any of her previous boyfriends. Not that he was her boyfriend or anything, but still, this was supposed to be a date.

"It's okay. You can ask me anything. And no, I've never brought a date here. And to be fair, my 'dates' were usually just, ah…" His eyes widened slightly as he trailed off and started messing with his carabiner.

Yeah, she didn't need him to finish that since she could figure out what he'd been about to say anyway. He'd had a life before her, but she didn't need certain details. "All right, so tell me how we do this. If I slip off the wall, am I going to break anything or plummet to the ground?"

"Nope. You take this one step at a time, reaching for the climbing hold nearest your hand. It's easy if you have a level head—which you do. It's not a race, so we just get to the top when we get there. And then we'll basically rappel down very slowly. These ropes are set up to tighten and hold if you start falling, so you won't have to worry about ending up in a free fall or anything. Are you ready?"

"Ready." She just hoped her heart was ready for more because it was pretty clear that was where things were headed with the two of them.

Whether she wanted to put the brakes on or not, she could see the writing on the wall.

Excitement and fear warred inside her but she was going to let excitement win. Logan was worth it.

Chapter 16

"Success!" Grace pumped her fist in the air as she put on the go-kart's brakes. Then she turned around to grin at Logan, who was trailing behind her in his own go-kart. "I see you finally caught up, slacker."

"You were shockingly savage out there," he said laughingly. "So...you actually *are* competitive."

"Like I said, only when it's something I'm good at. And I just destroyed you."

"Cutting me off like a total lunatic seems a little unsportsmanlike." His grin was firmly in place as he jumped out of his go-kart.

She shrugged and jumped out of hers. "You're learning new things about me." It had been fun to speed around the little racecourse with no one else around. Rick had turned on the spotlights and there were plenty of lights from a nearby mini-golf course anyway.

He strode toward her, looking like a sexy, lethal predator. "Rick texted me, said we could just leave from here if we want. Unless you want to head back in?"

"I'm good. I'm kind of hungry too."

"I'm glad you said that. There's a little Italian place a couple blocks over. We can just walk if you want?"

"Perfect." The truth was, pretty much everything about him and this date was perfect. Her mind started to wander toward the future and what-ifs, but she ignored those thoughts. For once, she wanted to live in the moment, to enjoy this.

They stepped over the fence that extended around the go-kart area into the parking lot and Logan waved at one of the security cameras. "How does this rank as far as first dates go?" he murmured, slipping his hand into hers so smoothly.

She loved how openly affectionate he was, and tried not to compare him to her ex. But it was hard because Logan was wonderful in so many ways. And that terrified her. He seemed almost too good to be true. With her free hand, she tapped her lips with her finger. "Well, it's not over so I'm going to have to hold off on rating it just yet."

His eyes narrowed slightly. "Is that right?"

She shrugged, not bothering to hide her grin as he led them to his truck.

"Hmm, what can I do to make it the best first date you've ever had?"

"We'll see how your kissing skills are when you take me home." They'd kissed before, but she was going to tease him a little. She wasn't sure where the words were coming from, but she loved the way he slightly jolted as he opened his door.

"I'll try not to disappoint," he murmured. "You need your purse?" he asked.

"Yeah, thanks. And I'm paying for dinner tonight."

He snorted as he handed her purse over and shut the door. "I'm paying."

"Don't be difficult." She looped her purse over her body at a cross angle.

"I asked you out on a date," he murmured. "I'm paying." Taking her by surprise, he pinned her up against the door as he shut it, his gaze molten hot. "And I don't want to wait to kiss you." His words were harsh and raspy.

"So don't." She didn't want to wait either. Maybe she'd regret this later, but she didn't think so. And she had to stop fighting this thing between them, had to let her guard down a little.

That was all the encouragement he needed. Cupping her cheek, he slanted his mouth over hers, his tongue playful and teasing as he deepened the kiss.

She leaned into him, going from zero to a hundred just like that. Or maybe it wasn't so sudden. They'd been building to this all night—for weeks, even. She'd been having so much fun with him, but there'd been an underlying heat simmering the whole time just waiting to boil over.

And now she wasn't hungry for food at all, didn't care about heading to that restaurant. The only thing she wanted was more of Logan MacNeil.

When he slid a hand down her hip and moved it around her body, cupping her ass, she rolled her hips into his. This might technically be their first date but she already knew what was underneath his clothes and she wanted more.

So much more.

She nipped his bottom lip, earning a growl of appreciation from him. As she slid her hands up his chest—

A bright light illuminated them, startling her as an engine revved.

"What the hell?" Logan jerked back then stepped in front of her, blocking her from the spotlights.

"What's going on?" she asked, looking around him and shielding her eyes. "Did Rick turn on the—"

Lights blinded her as the sound of squealing tires filled the air. Her stomach tightened as Logan grabbed her hand and pulled. She didn't think, just ran with him across the parking lot as a vehicle raced at them.

The engine roared wildly over the erratic beat of her heart. She didn't dare look back because she was afraid of falling.

Logan's grip on her hand was tight as he dragged her forward.

Crunch!

As they dove over the fence to the go-karts, the loud sound of metal meeting metal rent the air. Her knees slammed against the concrete even as she allowed herself a quick glance back.

A truck had rammed into Logan's and was reversing.

"Keep going!" Logan yanked her to her feet and they ran across the racecourse. "We're almost there!" Logan's voice managed to get through to her over the loud rush of blood in her ears, over the fear eating away at her as they ran from the lunatic destroying Logan's truck.

As they reached the arcade doors, Rick swung one open, his eyes wide.

"I've called the cops! Saw that crazy driver on the security cameras. Are you guys okay?" He shut and locked it behind them.

"We're fine." Logan's voice was clipped as he pulled out his own phone and started making a call.

Grace finally turned to look out the glass doors and could see the taillights of the truck swerving out of the parking lot like a bat out of hell. Breathing hard, she forced herself to take slow, steadying breaths as she tried to get her heart rate under control.

What the hell had just happened?

CHAPTER 17

"I don't like that this has happened twice." Detective Hurley's expression was grim as he looked between the two of them. "It's not feeling like random violence anymore."

Yeah, no kidding, Logan thought. Sitting on a bench inside the now fully lit arcade, he scooted closer to Grace as they spoke to the detective.

Grace wrapped her arms around herself so Logan curled his arm around her shoulders. Some lunatic had tried to run them over while they'd been making out in the parking lot. That was some seriously psycho shit. Violent and unstable. Grace leaned into him, her slender frame trembling slightly, and he wanted to pummel whoever had done this.

"Thank you for coming down here," Logan said. He'd called Hurley directly even though Rick had said he was calling the cops. Because Logan's gut was telling him this and the drive-by at his house were connected, no matter that there had been a string of drive-by shootings. He simply didn't believe in coincidences like that. And both times he'd been with Grace when something had happened.

"I want to dig deeper into both of your personal lives," the detective said. "Logan, I've already dug pretty deep into yours and I checked again on the way here. Brister is still under supervision. He hasn't left Montana."

"You're sure?" Logan knew the detective would have done his due diligence, but he wanted more details. He hated not being in control of this situation. "I know you checked. I'm just..." He rubbed a hand over his head.

He hated that Grace had been put in danger again, that someone had come at the two of them because he'd been so damn distracted. He didn't want to get caught up in blaming himself but he should have been better aware of his surroundings. Should have protected her better. This incident never should have happened.

"I made contact with the sheriff up there. His deputy said Brister hasn't left his property. So there's no way he got from Montana to here in an hour." The detective looked at Grace. "I know we touched on some surface stuff, but can you think of anyone you might have had bad interactions with lately? Maybe at school? An angry parent? An ex-boyfriend? Maybe an altercation while you were out shopping or at your gym, or literally anything you can think of. At this point nothing is unimportant."

Grace shook her head. "No. I've never had an issue with a parent at school. My job is literally to help everyone who comes to me. And no run-ins while I'm driving or at a store... Nothing that could warrant this kind of escalating behavior."

"You ran into your ex-fiancé a month ago," Logan murmured.

She shot him a surprised look. Then she looked back to the detective and nodded. "I did run into my ex-fiancé with his new wife. Things were awkward but he's the one who left me. There's no animosity on his part. I haven't talked to him since I moved to Vegas, with the exception of the other night. Though..." She cleared her throat. "He did try to send me a message on social media. I filtered the message because I didn't want to read what he had to say. We're not friends online or anything and all my information is private. I can't imagine him trying to do this. It's not his personality, and what would be the point?"

Her ex reaching out to her was news to Logan, not that he expected Grace to tell him everything. Still, it annoyed him that the loser was sending her messages. He'd lost any right to contact her, to even say her name after what he'd done.

"When you get a chance I'd like you to read the message and let me know what it says. Even if it seems harmless, I'd like to analyze it," the detective said.

"Ah, okay. I can do it right now." She pulled out her phone and after a few moments of swiping across her screen, held it out to the detective.

He made a few notes and Logan was able to see that it was a fairly benign message, with the ex telling her she'd looked fantastic the other night and asking if she wanted to get together and catch up over drinks next time he was in town.

What a douche. Logan really did want to punch that guy in his face.

Once he was done, Hurley put his notepad away. "I've got my guys making copies of the security feeds, so hopefully we'll be able to get something. We're also checking security along the street to see if another camera picked something up. The main thing I can tell you right now is to be careful. And if you feel like it and are able, get away for a few days. If you do, let me know where you're going. We're going to catch whoever did this, but just be smart." He flicked a glance at Logan, his expression hard.

As if Logan would do any different. But he knew from his boss that this particular detective cared a lot. "I'll be staying with Grace for the foreseeable future. And as you know, I've increased security at my house. If anything shows up on one of my cameras, you're the first person I'll send the information to." A small lie, because he would definitely be sending it first to Vadim at the Serafina. In fact, as soon as they left here, he was calling his friend and coworker and giving him an update. Vadim would be able to hack any nearby CCTVs and hopefully figure out who was behind this before the cops did.

The sooner this was all over, the better. And Logan didn't care about breaking a few laws to find this guy and stop it before it escalated any further.

CHAPTER 18

Logan scrubbed a hand over his face as he poured a cup of coffee into one of Grace's mugs that said *I'm a school counselor, what's your superpower?* He and Grace had gotten in to her place late last night after all the questioning—and he'd stayed up even later talking to Vadim and digging into some potential former dates as threats. It seemed ridiculous because he hadn't gone on a date in so damn long and he'd never gotten serious with anyone, but he was covering everything at this point. His only priority was keeping Grace and himself safe from a lunatic.

His phone buzzed in his pocket, and he tensed when he saw Detective Hurley's name. "Hey."

"Are you with Grace?"

"She's still sleeping." And he wasn't going to wake her up. "I can relay anything to her. What's up?" Because this definitely wasn't a social call.

"Got a couple things for you. Neither of them great. Austin Brister? He's not where the sheriff's office said he was. I talked to the deputy in charge of keeping an eye on him last night and it turns out he's actually been MIA for a couple days. Apparently they assumed he went off on a bender because that's what some of the ranch hands *told* them. He'd damaged his ankle monitor—supposedly by accident—days ago and they're in the process of getting a new one. They were trying to keep it quiet, but with what happened last night they finally fessed up. And before you say anything, heads are going to roll because of this." There was more than a bite to Hurley's words. "We can't get a hit on his phone and he hasn't used his credit cards anywhere. Not in Montana, not here in Vegas."

Logan cursed. "Has someone let his wife know?"

"Yep. She's aware and so are the cops in her town so she'll have eyes on her sister's place for a while."

At least that was something, but he didn't like that the guy had gone completely dark. "You said you had a couple things?"

"Yeah. This is probably nothing. But I looked into Grace's ex-fiancé and he's currently in Vegas now too."

"He's here? Like on vacation?"

"Well I called him and it went to voicemail, so I did some digging and found his wife's phone number. When I asked to talk to him, she informed me that he hasn't been in contact with her for a solid week and she can't get a hold of him. She sounded more pissed than worried. I looked into his credit cards, and as of a few days ago a couple of charges popped up in Vegas. Which is why I think she was so angry. Apparently she tried to file a missing persons report and the detective told her the same thing. All his recent charges are in Vegas so he's alive, and not there under duress according to some ATM videos I grabbed. He hasn't done anything illegal that we know of, but we're looking to bring him in for questioning in case he's related to any of this."

"Thank you. I think I'm going to get out of town for a few days with Grace." If she agreed to go with him, because he wasn't leaving her. Finding out where she lived wouldn't be particularly hard if someone wanted to badly enough, and Logan wanted to have more control of their surroundings.

"That sounds like a good idea. Look man, I'm sorry this is happening right around Christmas."

"Not your fault. And I appreciate this heads-up. I know you don't have to give me these updates."

"No problem. Keep your head down."

"10-4." After they disconnected, he set his phone on the countertop and sighed.

"So we're taking a trip somewhere?" Grace stepped into the kitchen, looking half asleep with faint circles under her eyes telling him she hadn't slept well. She still looked adorable in blue pajamas with little white snowflakes all over them.

Once they'd arrived home last night he'd thought she might want to talk but she'd holed up in her room. And he didn't blame her. The attack was a lot to handle, especially for her—someone sweet and unused to violence.

"Sit, I'll get your coffee." He grabbed what he knew was her favorite mug and started doctoring her coffee the way she liked as she sat at the center island.

"Thank you," she murmured. "Now what's going on? You have a look like you don't want to tell me something. So if we're going to leave town, then I'm assuming it's not good."

He quickly went over everything Detective Hurley had just told him, and she sat there drinking her coffee silently, taking it all in.

"I almost guarantee that my ex is in Vegas simply because he likes it. It has nothing to do with me."

Logan lifted a shoulder and took a sip of his own coffee. "Maybe, maybe not. I don't like that he's here."

"I'm more worried about Brister," she murmured. "He beat his wife for years and you stopped him. I wish the cops could do more."

"Well that brings me to something else. I want you to pack a bag and we're going to head to the Serafina. Not to stay, but I work with someone who can dig a little deeper for us. I'm going to forward him this new information and I want to talk to him in person before we head out."

"Is this Angel's husband we're going to see?"

"Yes." Vadim was a hacker extraordinaire and had no problem working outside legal lines for a good cause.

Picking up her mug, Grace stood. "Christmas is in two days. If we head out now, you're going to miss spending it with your family."

"I know. But that's just the way it is." His family would sure as hell prefer them to stay alive and off the radar while the cops looked into this.

Setting her mug down, Grace rounded the island and pulled him into an unexpected hug. "I'm sorry you have to miss Christmas with your family."

He was sorry too, but... "At least I get to spend it with you." He kissed the top of her head, subtly inhaling her vanilla scent. Everything about the situation sucked but he would be with Grace at least.

That was the only silver lining.

She knew he wanted more from her, and even though their date had been interrupted, he was going to take advantage of the time they got to spend together. He was going to show her exactly how serious he was.

Because with Grace he couldn't just give her words. He had to use action. She'd been burned by a man who'd claimed to love her, who'd proposed to her. No, words wouldn't do for her.

CHAPTER 19

Grace held on to Logan's hand as they stepped off the elevator onto the fiftieth floor of the Serafina. She'd never been up here before and he'd had to use a specific key card to access the floor, bypassing all others. She felt a little out of place as they passed various men and women wearing sharp-looking black pants, black jackets and crisp white button-downs. Though none of them wore overt nametags saying they worked here, it was all very uniform.

In contrast, she was wearing jeans, ankle boots, and a long-sleeved peasant blouse with oversized hoop earrings and a jangle of bracelets. She'd left her jacket in Logan's rental truck.

As they approached two glass doors in the middle of a whole wall of tinted glass, they immediately swished open, letting them into what turned out to be a huge security area.

She looked around in fascination at the wall of video screens as a low hum of voices filled the air. She'd known that of course the casino had something like this, but seeing it in person was even more impressive than she'd imagined.

Iris Christiansen—a fierce and tall, stunning woman who Grace knew was the head of security and one of Logan's bosses—strode up to them and gave Grace a small smile. "Grace, good to see you again, though I wish it was under different circumstances." She briefly shook hands with Logan before motioning that they should follow her.

Moments later they were in a huge office with a wall of windows overlooking the city, making the space seem even bigger than it was.

Vadim looked up from the bank of computers at his desk—which had a cute picture of Angel and him on their wedding day—and nodded at Logan before smiling warmly at Grace. He stood from his desk and gave her a quick hug, which seemed to surprise Logan, if his frown was any indication. She wasn't sure why though—Logan knew they were friendly.

"It's good to see you," she said as he sat back down. "Angel texted me a picture of what you got her for Christmas. It's beautiful." The man had given his wife a gorgeous necklace with an angel charm made of diamonds and rose gold. Apparently he hadn't been able to wait until Christmas. Which made him that much more adorable.

He rubbed the back of his head. "I'm just glad she likes it."

"Oh she loves it. She's been showing it off to everyone."

This seemed to please him more. He cleared his throat and motioned toward his desk. "I looked into what you told me," he said to Logan before focusing all his attention on the screens and his keyboard.

Grace watched in fascination as various images popped up, both of her ex, Kevin, and of Austin Brister.

"I can't find anything on Brister here in Vegas. Though to be more specific, no images here in Vegas but also no images anywhere else recently. So it's possible he's holed up somewhere and going on a bender like his people in Montana seem to think. It's hard to fall off-grid completely and not get picked up on any cameras."

"What about Kevin?" Logan stepped closer, his jaw tight as his gaze swept over the screens.

"Well, this is pretty interesting." An image popped up of her ex-fiancé leaving a strip club with a tall, dark-haired woman who looked a bit like Grace.

"This is the last image I have of him. Through some digging I found out who the woman is so I'm going to send someone by her house," he said, motioning to the screen. "See if we can get eyes on him. He could be at her place, or it's possible they hooked up and now he's sleeping it off in a cash-only motel. There are a lot of cameras in Vegas and I haven't captured his image on any in the last six hours, which tells me he's lying low in one place as of right now. Hell, he could be in another strip club."

Logan nodded and stepped back, taking Grace's hand in his again. She liked that he was publicly claiming her like this, as if he was proud to be with her.

"Thank you for that," Logan said. I've got my phone on me and so does Grace. We're heading out of town but we'll be available if you need anything."

"Stay safe. Are you taking extra precautions?" Vadim stood, pushing his chair back.

"Of course."

Grace wondered exactly what extra precautions he meant, though she had an idea. She knew Logan had a concealed weapon permit for his job and that he often carried a weapon. It was kind of weird for her, but she understood it was his job.

"Good. Call if you need anything," Vadim said, looking between her and Logan.

"I'll walk you guys out," Iris said as Vadim returned to his desk.

Grace wasn't sure where they were going, but knowing that the people Logan worked with were working on this mess, as well as the police, made her feel a whole lot better.

She just wanted this nightmare over, wanted to go back to her normal life. The only silver lining in all this garbage was that she'd get to spend time with Logan.

CHAPTER 20

"You don't have to keep turning around," Logan murmured. He knew Grace was edgy but soon they'd be out of the city limits and away from the threat. He hoped that during this time together he'd be able to solidify their relationship.

Even though he wanted a more active role in bringing down whoever was behind the two attacks on them—and his money was on Brister—his priority had to be keeping Grace safe. The police were good at their jobs and Vadim was a magician. Logan had to trust the process.

Sighing, Grace turned around in the passenger seat and faced forward. "I know. I'm just feeling off-kilter, I guess."

"I get it. But I've been keeping an eye on the rearview mirror and haven't seen a car for the last five miles. And Iris had one of our team scan my rental truck for any sort of trackers while we were up talking to Vadim. Trust me, no one knows where this place is."

"Including me." There was a slight touch of humor in her voice. "So where is this place, anyway?"

"A house out in the desert. Not exactly off-grid, but a few miles away from any main roads. Not in a neighborhood, and about twenty minutes away from anything resembling a grocery store. A buddy of mine owns it and he's currently overseas."

"Okay, that sounds pretty nice. Maybe we'll even be able to put up a little Christmas tree or something?"

He heard the wistfulness in her voice and was glad he'd packed a few extra supplies in the cab of the truck. He wanted to surprise her, however, so he didn't tell her what he'd brought. "Sounds like a plan. So how are you dealing with everything? Seriously."

"Good enough. And I honestly don't want to talk about it. I'm trying to sort of mentally process it all first, and I'm a big believer in distraction. So tell me what's going on with you and your family. What do your parents say about all this?"

He lifted a shoulder and took a left-hand turn. "They don't like what's going on, obviously, but they really are fine with us leaving. They're concerned for us more than anything and just want us to stay safe. They know this is the best option right now. I just hate worrying them." His parents had done that enough, considering both their sons had been overseas on many deployments.

"I bet. So whatever happened with Brister's wife? Have you found out where she ended up, how she's doing?" Grace asked.

"She decided to leave her husband and is officially divorcing him. Apparently all her kids are out of the house now and she's staying with her sister. Her daughter is nearby too. Wyatt let me know yesterday that the divorce is going to be proceeding accordingly. She wants a settlement, but nothing to do with the ranch. In the end they'll both get a lot of money. So really, he's not getting screwed."

He lifted a shoulder even as his rage ratcheted up.

"I wish the guy would get taken to the cleaners, but that's not how life works. And it sounds as if she just wants to be free of him, not to ruin his life—which is pretty generous, if you ask me. I don't understand why he would want to come after me when he's the one who beat his own wife." And he was keeping his damn ranch, his money. Sure, he'd lost his wife, but that was his own fault. Brister had hurt the woman he should have been protecting.

Grace snorted softly. "You're an easy target. An actual physical one. And you're easy to blame. He doesn't want to look at himself in the mirror and take responsibility for his own actions. Coward," she muttered.

"Yeah, I know the reasoning. I just can't wrap my head around it."

"If more people would take responsibility for their actions, the world would be a better place," Grace murmured.

Wasn't that the truth. "So you really don't think your ex is in Vegas for anything to do with all this?" he asked quietly. He hated bringing the guy up, but since they were on the subject of Brister, he figured he might as well. It made him feel more in control to be focusing on the threats, and maybe there was something Grace hadn't thought of yet.

"No. I mean, I can't understand why he would, to be honest. But I am surprised that he potentially ditched his wife for a stripper in Vegas. It feels like such a cliché."

"The guy *is* a walking cliché," Logan muttered. He really would love to punch the guy in the face. Or the dick. "The woman from the video had a similar look to you, not his wife."

Grace simply shrugged. "So? Look, after things imploded between us, I found out he'd been hooking up with a woman he worked with, who looked nothing like me or his wife. Because he wasn't cheating with the woman he's now married to. The woman he worked with reached out to me on social media and confessed everything. I think she felt bad about the wedding falling apart. I'm not sure and I really don't care. Allegedly he always used condoms, but I still got checked out. Thankfully he didn't give me anything."

"Yep, I really want to punch him in the face," he muttered, seething inside.

"What?"

"Sorry, didn't mean to say that out loud." But he did mean the words.

Grace snickered, the sweet sound making his heart flip over. He loved it when she smiled or laughed. The woman could light up a room. "Well, he would be no match for you, that's for sure. And in the end he did me a favor. Cheating aside, because I never would have put up with that if I'd known, we never would have lasted. And I would have been miserable trying to fit myself into this mold of what he wanted instead of actually being myself."

The more she told him, the more Logan wondered why she'd even been with the guy in the first place. "Do you mind if I ask why you were with him at all? You're one of the most independent, smartest women I know."

Her cheeks flushed slightly. "Thanks," she murmured. "And it's not really one thing. He was very charming. He really knew how to turn it on. Especially in the beginning. But he had this way of making me feel bad about myself even when complimenting me. It was like I was constantly struggling to get his approval, which in hindsight is stupid because I don't need it. I never did. But..." She shrugged. "As you know, humans are very complicated. I'm just glad I got out before we actually got married. And if he hadn't blown off our wedding...I might not have even gone through with it. I was having a panic attack the morning of the wedding."

"Seriously?"

"Yep."

"Your instinct was telling you to run."

"Oh yeah. And I like to think I would have listened to it."

He was so damn glad he'd met Grace, so glad she was rid of that loser. Logan couldn't imagine his life without her.

"How much farther is this place?" she asked. "Not that I'm not enjoying the company."

"About ten minutes out." He subtly glanced in the rearview mirror now, the tension banded around his chest easing. Still no one on the road.

Soon he'd have Grace safe and away from the threat. This place had no link to either of them. They should be able to relax and just be together. And then he hoped to convince her that he wanted more than just dating. He wanted forever.

CHAPTER 21

Grace waited in the foyer as Logan looked around the house. He'd disarmed the security system but he'd still wanted to do a quick sweep of his friend's home. He was very thorough, she would give him that.

And at that thought, an unexpected rush of heat spread through her as she remembered exactly how *thorough* he'd been a month ago.

Glancing around the open space of the foyer, which connected right into the wide-open living room, she loved how much natural light was flooding in. Everything was wood and stone and she loved the rustic-looking beams that ran the length of the living room ceiling. Not to mention that the huge bay of windows lining one wall made her feel like she was outside with nature. Since it was cold she was glad she wasn't actually outside, but it was a pretty incredible design. His friend was clearly doing all right for himself.

"The place is good," Logan said, stepping into the living room. "I'm going to grab our stuff from the truck. There are two bedrooms straight through there," he said motioning to the left of the living room where a short hallway shot off. "The second one is bigger, so you take that one. But feel free to join me in my room any time you want." Despite the situation, he gave her one of his wicked signature grins.

After what they'd been dealing with, she was feeling bold. And she was done not going for what she wanted. Maybe she'd get her heart broken, but she had to take a chance. "Why don't we both take the bigger bedroom?"

He stopped in his tracks, staring at her for a long moment. Instead of looking smug, he went all hot and smoldering. He looked as if he wanted to say more, but only paused before he headed out of the house to grab their stuff.

Well, good. Because she hadn't been kidding. Maybe she would regret the offer if she gave him her all and things didn't work out, but she didn't think so. She wasn't sure how long they were going to be here, and screw it—she wasn't sleeping alone tonight. She wasn't going to deprive herself. Or Logan, for that matter. They'd crossed into more-than-friends territory a month ago and she was going to have to risk her heart at this point. Even if she was nervous.

Since he'd already cleared the house, she decided to go exploring and check everything out.

The kitchen was the same as the living room area with lots of wood and stone and sturdy quartz countertops. And again with the huge windows overlooking the snowcapped mountains in the distance. It was so gorgeous and felt so isolated that she couldn't believe how close they were to Vegas. It was like they were in the middle of nowhere in this desert space. She easily imagined that at night it would be gorgeous with the stars and moon overhead. And with a fire crackling and a sexy man to enjoy the evening with? Yeah, pretty damn nice.

As she glanced around the kitchen, she realized she hadn't thought of food. So she hoped Logan had remembered to bring something. Because she was terribly unprepared; all she'd thought to grab was a bag of clothing and toiletries. She'd also brought her laptop so she could keep in touch with her boss if necessary, but she really hoped this mess was over before school started back up.

"Everything's in the living room," Logan said as he stepped into the kitchen, a couple bags in hand. "And I just got off the phone with Roman—they've installed cameras at your place."

She blinked in surprise. "Seriously?" That fast?

"Yep. It was an easy install. All wireless, so basically he just had to screw the cameras in place and program them to the app." He started pulling out food-stuffs—thankfully he *had* come prepared—so she helped him unpack the various boxes and bags. "He's going to keep an eye on my place and your place in case anything happens. I'll get you the app info so you can download it to your phone and you can check on the cameras anytime you want to. Whoever is behind this will pay."

There was a bite to his tone that reminded her he had a whole lot of training to back up his words. It was sexy and intimidating. "So I know we didn't talk about it, and I know Vadim is apparently really good with computers, considering all that stuff he did earlier," she said. "That was all...super illegal, right?"

Logan simply snorted. "Let's just say I'm glad I'm friends with him. If he wanted, he could destroy someone's life."

"That's a little terrifying. I guess I always viewed him as this mushy teddy bear because I've only ever seen him with Angel up until today. He seemed so much more serious and intense in his office."

Logan laughed now. "A mushy teddy bear. I'm totally going to tell him that."

Grace didn't care because Vadim was sweet and she loved the way he was with Angel. It was so clear to anyone who saw them together how much he loved his wife.

"So I guess we're just sitting tight, or can we explore a little and go hiking around here?" There didn't seem to be much nearby except rugged red rocks, tons of cacti and a lot of thick, green and brown underbrush. Even so, she liked the desolate beauty of the land surrounding them.

"Before dark I actually do want to scope out the land," he said as he shut the refrigerator. "I've been here before but I still want to refresh my memory and check things out."

"Sounds good to me." She knew they were going to be here for a while, at least until whoever was behind everything was caught. Plus...she knew that as soon as Logan made the move they were very likely going to be having sex. A lot of it, if history was going to repeat itself. She'd told him what she wanted so it was up to him at this point. Her boldness only went so far.

Before that, she needed to center herself more. Nerves danced through her and she needed to stretch her legs, to walk off some of this wild energy pulsing through her. Because once they crossed that line, there was no going back.

Who was she kidding? They'd already crossed that line a month ago.

They were long past the point of no return.

CHAPTER 22

Grace breathed in the crisp, dry desert air as Logan walked ahead of her. He'd told her that his friend was out of the country and knew they were staying at his place. The man had a cleaning service that came in once a week to keep up with dust, but he'd put them on hold while Grace and Logan were here. So no one should be nearby.

Huge cacti and underbrush were thick around the property, beautiful in a wild sort of way. She knew in about four months there would be tons of purples, pinks and yellows with the wildflowers that grew out here. For now, the red from the clay earth and rocks was the only spot of color as they trekked along the well-worn path. Though maybe path was an exaggeration. A rocky, dusty walkway that was just big enough for one person at a time extended around the whole property, according to Logan, stretching on for a couple miles before looping back to the house.

He was about twenty feet ahead of her, scouting for potential danger—though he thankfully didn't expect any out here.

Since no one knew where they were, some of her tension had eased. Though not all of it, considering they couldn't go home and so much was in the air until the police figured out who was behind everything.

But at least she was with Logan. He had a way of making everything seem better, of making her feel safe even with all the craziness that had happened. He always had a positive attitude about things, which was a refreshing change from her ex.

Again, she hated that she was comparing the two, but damn, it was so hard not to. It was like comparing night and day. Sure, Logan had a reputation as a player but...she was going with her instinct. He'd been so honest with her and was always kind to those around him. Her especially.

He made her feel special and valued. And she totally needed to get out of her head right now.

Stepping over a rock jutting out from the side of the pathway, she looked up and smiled at Logan who was hacking away at some of the thick underbrush ahead. He'd shoved his sleeves up, showing off sexy, muscular forearms she wanted to stroke her fingers over.

He started to smile at her, but froze.

Immediately her heart rate kicked up and she glanced over her shoulder. Had someone found them here? *No, impossible.*

"Grace, listen to me carefully." Logan's voice carried through the quiet air.

Heart in her throat, she turned back to him and nodded, afraid to move.

"There's a big speckled rattlesnake to the right of you. It's blending in but I can see it from here. It is highly poisonous and it wasn't there when I passed by."

Her entire body flushed hot then cold as icy fingers scraped down her spine. Swallowing hard, she looked in the direction he'd indicated and saw the huge snake in a tight, round coil. Ready to strike.

"Take a step back. Slowly."

She did as he said, staring at the coiled-up snake. Heart racing in a staccato beat, she took another step back when the serpent uncoiled, lifting its head to stare right at her.

She felt frozen to the spot. She was vaguely aware of Logan moving toward her, his machete in hand as she took another step backward.

When the snake started shaking its tail, rattling wildly, sweat dotted her upper lip and down her back as she tried to force her legs to move faster.

Move. Move. Move.

She didn't want to bolt and freak the thing out, but all her instincts were screaming at her to sprint away for her life.

As she took another step back, then another, she lost her balance as she collided with the rock she'd jumped over before. "Shit!" She threw out her hands to stop herself as she tumbled backward.

The snake launched in her direction, the dry shaking of the rattle loud in her ears as she tumbled over the rock. A sharp pop of pain fractured through her shoulder as she rammed into another rock. Ignoring the pain, she rolled onto all fours and pushed up. Little pebbles dug into her palms as she shoved to her feet and stumbled back.

Swish. Swish.

By the time she managed to steady herself, Logan was standing over the dead snake, bloody machete in hand. She stared in shock for a long moment. She hadn't even seen him strike.

"Are you okay?" Logan leapt over the rock in one quick leap.

Wincing, she wiped her palms on her pants. "Yeah. Just a little dusty and I hit my shoulder." She'd feel it tomorrow for sure. But she hadn't been bitten by a poisonous snake, so she was taking the win.

He took one of her hands in his and frowned as he brushed away some little pebbles. "Looks like you got a few scrapes. Let's head back and clean you up."

"For some reason I wasn't even thinking about snakes." She shuddered as they headed back, realizing there was a whole lot of other wildlife out here. Cougars, coyotes, anything. "I think I'm going to stay inside the whole time we're here," she muttered.

To her surprise he didn't laugh, he simply squeezed her shoulder as he moved in behind her. "I think you deserve a hot bath and to relax."

"So do you," she said, looking over her shoulder at him.

His lips actually kicked up. "I'm not exactly a bath kind of person."

"Even if you have company?"

"Only if the company is you."

Oh damn.

He looked away, scanning their surroundings in the same intense way she'd seen him do since they arrived. He was always aware of everything, it seemed. Always ready to protect her.

His last words reached deep inside her, sending a push of warmth everywhere throughout her. She'd already trusted him with her body. It was definitely time to trust him with her heart.

A month of fantasizing and living on memories was at an end.

CHAPTER 23

Grace stepped out of the huge, masculine bedroom feeling a bit better. Logan had helped her clean up her hands once they'd gotten back to the house, and even though her shoulder was sore, the rock hadn't broken her skin at least. She could deal with a bruise. The shower, however, was the only reason she was feeling human right now.

In fresh lounge pants, a pullover sweater and with slightly damp hair, she entered the living room and her heart skipped a beat when she saw a small Christmas tree set up next to the electric fireplace. "What's all this?" she asked Logan as he strode into the room carrying a little brown bag.

"I was hoping to be done before you came out. I'm almost finished." He pulled a small ornament out of the bag and put the sparkly red ball on the tree.

Okay, how sweet was this? Her instinct was right on with this man. "Where did you get all this?"

"I actually brought it with me. I tucked it away in the back of the truck. I hate that you're missing Christmas, so I thought I'd bring it to you."

"You're the one missing it with your family." And his family was a whole lot better than hers. She'd planned to have Christmas dinner with a group of friends. Heck, she hadn't even talked to her mom about holiday plans, which was very much normal for the two of them. They rarely talked on the phone and she couldn't remember the last holiday they'd spent together. Maybe...when she'd been in high school.

"Like I said, I get to spend it with you." He shrugged and put a silver and white ornament on the tree.

Okay, she was officially melting.

Crossing the living room, she reached into the bag and pulled out an ornament, unable to miss that electric shock when their fingers grazed each other. "I'm glad I get to spend it with you too. The only thing we need to add to this is Christmas music."

Grinning, he handed her the bag and picked up a remote control from one of the side tables. Moments later soft instrumental music was playing from hidden speakers throughout the room.

Considering the tree was only four feet tall and already had a string of lights on, it didn't take long to put the rest of the ornaments on it. Once they finished, Logan plugged it in and she smiled at the cheerful, glittering display. It seemed brighter, homier, next to the fireplace, and the sight made her long for something she'd never had. Something she wanted with Logan.

To her horror, tears suddenly sprang to her eyes.

Logan let out a soft curse as he cupped her cheeks, swiping away the few errant tears that spilled over. "Don't cry," he said quietly.

"These are happy tears, I promise. Or they're a mix, I guess. I'm just feeling really overwhelmed and emotional right now. And what you did, that you thought to even bring a tree and ornaments, is incredibly sweet. More than sweet. You're so wonderful." The words came out a little like an accusation because he was breaking down all her barriers. Simply knocking them down like they were dominoes and she was powerless to protect herself from it.

"Grace," he murmured, then paused, as if he wanted to say more. Instead he dipped his head, moving slowly, giving her time to stop him.

Nope. The chance to stop this train had passed. And she didn't want to put the brakes on anyway. She'd been fighting this for too long, trying to take baby steps with him. Well, screw baby steps. She was still a little afraid of being hurt, but she didn't want to miss her chance. And this felt like the start of something new for them.

As he slanted his mouth over hers something inside her snapped free. She flashed back on the night in the hotel room as he'd slid his tongue inside her mouth, teasing, testing, making her want him even more. When he'd pressed her up against the shower wall, water pulsing around them as he'd thrust into her, over and over. All those naked memories were at the forefront of her brain and she wanted it all over again. Wanted him so bad she was practically trembling with the need.

Leaning into him, she linked her fingers together behind his neck, holding on for dear life.

At the same time he deepened their kiss, pressing his body against hers even as she lifted her leg and wrapped it around him—as if she was going to climb him like a damn tree. Which sounded like a good idea.

Even though the temperature in the room was perfect, she felt too hot, too needy, too something. She wanted him inside her right now, wanted to feel joy and pleasure and she wanted it with him. Only him. She'd completely fallen for him and there was no sense in denying it to herself any longer.

As if he'd read her mind, or maybe just sensed her mood, he pulled back a fraction. "Here or the bedroom?" he growled out, the words raspy and unsteady.

Oh, they were definitely on the same page. They were getting naked and she couldn't wait until they got to the bedroom. It was too far.

"Here." Right on the floor. Or the couch. She didn't care. She just wanted a flat surface and him inside her. Feeling manic with hunger for him, she jumped up, wrapping her legs around him as he groaned into her mouth.

He easily held her as he knelt down on the soft, fluffy rug stretched out in front of the fireplace. The man had such an incredible, raw strength and it was a huge turn-on.

She arched her hips into him as he tugged her sweater off. Her lounge pants went next, a blur of cotton material tossed to the side—and she hadn't bothered with panties. Maybe because she'd hoped this would happen. But when he would have dipped his head between her legs, she grabbed onto his T-shirt. She wanted him, but it was her turn to see what she'd been missing.

"No way. I've been fantasizing about that body for a month." She grinned at the surprise playing on his face. "That can't really be a shock, can it?"

"Well I am pretty incredible," he murmured, tugging his shirt off and revealing that eight-pack she'd had dirty dreams about. "But I guarantee your fantasies have nothing on mine. I've been obsessed. I've been jerking off to thoughts of you every damn night for the last month."

A shiver trailed down her spine at his words. Obsessed? Yeah, she was right there too. And it scared the hell out of her. What happened if he got bored with her or realized she wasn't really special at all?

Noooo. She shut down that annoying, bullshit insecurity that wanted to bubble up inside her and reached for the button of his pants. He was here with her now because he wanted to be. And when he looked at her, it was as if she was the only person who existed for him. She needed to let go of her own bullshit, just throw it away.

When she couldn't get his button free he took over and tugged his pants off, but not before grabbing a condom. Thankfully one of them was thinking clearly because her brain had basically turned into mush.

"On your back first," she rasped out. She wanted to taste him, had been thinking about it for a while. She wanted to get him worked up and so crazy with lust for her, just the way she was for him. And she loved how he groaned when she went down on him. That sound alone was empowering and heady.

He paused but laid back, stretching out like a god in front of her. His erection was thick and heavy, jutting forward and begging for her to touch.

Kneeling in between his legs, she couldn't bite back her own groan as she wrapped her fingers around his hard length. "I've been masturbating to the memory of you too," she whispered as she stroked him once, long and firm.

He shuddered. "Fuuuuck. You are really good for my ego."

Smiling at that, she leaned forward and slowly, gently licked the underside of his shaft. He'd teased her more than once and she was going to do the same to him.

He cursed, clutching the big rug underneath them instead of sliding his fingers through her hair like she'd expected.

Maybe he was still trying to hold on to his control. Well, she was going to make him lose it. Continuing to tease him, she rubbed his thick length against her cheek, loved exactly how silky-soft his cock was on her skin.

"Killing me," he growled. "Such a pretty, fucking tease."

She smiled at the tremble in his voice and teased the head of his cock with her tongue. His thigh muscles tightened and his breathing kicked up.

Oh, she was getting him there all right. Without warning, she sucked him into her mouth, *deep*.

"Grace." He groaned out her name like a prayer and she liked how powerful it made her feel. She loved getting this big, wonderful man all worked up for her. She hated the reason they were here, but she was glad that it was just the two of them right now. Glad they could enjoy and explore each other with no interruptions and no outside world bothering them.

Dipping her head again, she continued teasing him, over and over, pulling him deep into her mouth. He trembled underneath her until he suddenly grabbed her shoulders.

She lifted her head, looking up the length of his work-of-art body. "What?"

"I'm not coming in your mouth this time." His dark eyes were filled with heat, all for her. "I've waited too long."

She'd barely nodded before he had her flat on her back and underneath him, all that power pulsing against her. God, the man was incredible. She loved the feel of all his hard muscles on top of her, pushing her down against the rug.

He crushed his mouth over hers as he stretched out fully on top of her, cupping her mound and gently teasing a finger along her slick folds, but not penetrating. He didn't even wait, just went straight for where she wanted him most.

And yeah, she was definitely wet for him. How could she not be? The hot pulse between her legs was a constant and only he could ease her ache.

He groaned into her mouth and started kissing a scorching path along her jawline before nibbling on her ear.

He knew how much that drove her crazy, that barely there bite that sent shivers spiraling throughout her. She arched up into him, clutching his shoulders tightly. All the muscles in her body were pulled taut with anticipation because she knew what was coming. Knew how thick he was and how incredible he felt thrusting inside her. She'd been fantasizing about it for a month.

She rolled her hips against his hand and he immediately slid a finger inside her.

Her inner walls tightened around him but his finger was definitely not enough. It took the edge off a little, however, as he continued his teasing kisses down her body.

He took his time with her breasts as she slid her fingers through his thick hair, holding him close.

"More." It came out half demand, half plea. She needed more than this, something he no doubt understood.

Making a regretful sound, he pulled away from her rock-hard nipple and kept going, not stopping until he was between her legs.

Placing his hands on her inner thighs, he stared down at her sex as if she was a Christmas present. In that moment, something inside her shifted.

Seriously, this man completely owned her heart. *Why* had she been fighting this? She knew the answer but it wasn't important. Not now, not in this space between them. Not when he deserved all of her focus.

He dipped his head between her legs and oh so gently, *too gently*, flicked his tongue against her clit. It wasn't nearly enough pressure.

"Who's the tease now?" she growled. All her muscles trembled, her inner walls tightening around his finger, and she needed so much more.

He chuckled against her sensitive skin. "You love it," he murmured.

She did. Waaaaaay too much. "Foreplay later. It's been a whole month. I need to take the edge off."

He flicked her clit again, still not with enough pressure. "This is payback for destroying me at the arcade." He chuckled again, the sound reverberating through her.

Despite how tense she was, how tight her muscles were, she found herself laughing as well. She'd never really laughed during sex before, not like she did with Logan.

He could be intense and serious but he also knew not to take himself so seriously. He was such a breath of fresh air and fun even in the bedroom. He was wonderful everywhere. What she saw with him was what she got. No lies, no pretenses. Just Logan.

Without warning, he slid another finger inside her just as he started flicking his tongue harder against her sensitive bundle of nerves.

Oh yeah, that's it. He'd learned her body so damn well, so damn *fast*. "Logan." His name tore from her throat.

That seemed to spur him on so she said his name again. And again. Every time she did, he gave her exactly what she needed. Harder and faster.

She was so close to coming, but she tightened her fingers against his head. "I'm close... I want you in me." Did she ever.

Growling against her, he quickly drew back, but only for a moment to grab a condom. In seconds he sheathed himself before stretching out on top of her, all raw power.

She trailed her fingers over his hard shoulders and biceps, relearning the feel of him after a month of having only her fantasies. He might not be hers forever, but he was hers right now and she was going to enjoy the hell out of him. Out of them. They fit so well together, especially like this. There was so much damn chemistry it rattled her.

He looked down at her with such intensity, as if he wanted to say something more, but instead he nudged her slick entrance with his thick erection.

She rolled her hips up to meet him just as he thrust forward. Letting her head fall back, she sucked in a breath as he thrust harder.

That was exactly the spot.

He kissed and teased along her neck, nibbling as he drove into her, the dichotomy of the featherlight kisses and his hard thrusts making her crazy.

"Come for me," he growled, even as he reached between their bodies and rubbed her clit.

She was already so close to release that when he stroked her it unleashed the tide of building pleasure.

Her climax punched through her as she wrapped her body around his, digging her fingers into his back and meeting him stroke for stroke.

He growled something against her neck that she couldn't understand but it didn't matter. Nothing mattered except pleasure right now. Hers and Logan's.

As she found release, he kept moving inside her and she could tell the moment before he was going to come.

"Grace," he rasped out right before all his muscles tightened, his body trembling against hers.

She reached down to grab his ass, clutching him hard as he found his own release in long, hard strokes. Her own orgasm kept going until she finally collapsed against the rug, her heart still a wild beat.

Breathing hard, he caged her in with his forearms, looking down at her with a mix of satisfaction and something raw and hungry in his expression. "We should have been doing this for weeks," he murmured before nipping her bottom lip.

"Maybe," she whispered teasingly, laughing lightly at her absurdity.

He bit her bottom lip between his teeth. "No maybe. And we are so not done," he said as he eased out of her. He quickly disposed of the condom then scooped her up from the rug. "We're going to find a bed right now."

Satisfied and lethargic, she curled into him. The crackling warmth from the electric fireplace was romantic, especially since it was right next to the cute little tree he'd put up, but a bed sounded pretty damn good right about now.

She forced herself not to think of the future, of what this meant for them, of anything other than his rock-hard body against hers and the time they were getting to spend together. After the last week, they deserved to simply enjoy themselves.

She would have to face reality soon enough.

CHAPTER 24

Feeling refreshed despite the lingering ball of tension at the base of her spine, Grace stepped out of the bedroom and was greeted with the smell of...was that bacon? Oh, yes, Merry Christmas-ish indeed. And now she would forgive Logan for making her wake up alone.

This was definitely the weirdest Christmas Eve she'd ever had—being in hiding was just plain surreal—but bacon and hopefully sex again soon was a good way to start it. And she really hoped coffee was already made too. It was chilly so she'd tugged on some thick socks and one of Logan's sweaters. It hung to mid-thigh and she loved his smell surrounding her.

She grinned as she stepped into the kitchen. "You look good in an apron."

He grinned right back and slid a couple pieces of bacon onto a paper-towel-covered plate. "And you look good in my sweater." He stepped away from the stove for a moment to brush his lips over hers. Almost immediately he deepened the kiss and she leaned into it, pressing her body up against his. He only pulled back as grease popped loudly. "Get coffee and sit. I'll serve you. And Merry Christmas Eve."

"The same to you too." She really wished she'd brought his present now. "You know, I could get used to you cooking all the time. It's incredibly hot."

"Good thing I like to cook."

"Seriously?" She poured a mug of coffee, inhaling the rich scent.

"Yeah, my dad did most of the cooking and I guess I just picked that up from him. He loves cooking for my mom. Which is good, because she sucks at it."

His parents really were the cutest and had been together forever, it seemed. A little pang hit her in the chest as she wondered what that would be like, to be with someone that long. To have an actual partner in everything. To have Logan as her partner. "I might hold on to you if you keep this up," she murmured before taking a sip of the hot brew. Her words were teasing, but she wasn't kidding. She wanted to keep him for always.

"If I'd known that the way to your heart was that easy, I'd have started cooking for you a long time ago." He surprised her by moving up behind her and leaning down to kiss her neck quickly before stepping back to the stove.

More warmth spread through her as she sat at the center island. She wasn't used to such casual affection like this. Even with her ex, things had never been so relaxed and easy as they were with Logan. And Kevin had never once cooked for her. Commented on how much she ate, sure, but cooked? No.

On that thought she decided not to think about her ex at all today. He didn't deserve space in her head. Not after everything she'd shared with Logan. Because Logan was one of a kind.

"Where did you even get bacon?"

"My brother got someone on the security team to do a delivery about an hour ago. Just a few more basic things we might need over the next week, and this makes it easy to stay put."

"Is that safe? Him bringing stuff by, I mean?"

"It should be. I'm not friends with the guy who dropped everything off. No one after me should be watching him for any reason. Wyatt paid him extra to do this so I don't feel too bad that he's running errands."

The tension that had started to build eased at his words. "Okay, then. If you're not worried, then I'm not either." Well, not too much, because she couldn't help some fear. There was someone out there who wanted to hurt one or both of them.

"I hope you're hungry, because I cooked a lot of bacon."

"Those are the sexiest words you've ever said to me."

He laughed, the rich sound rolling over her as he put a few pieces onto a plate and slid it in front of her. "I would ask if you want some fresh fruit, but I know what you're going to say."

She grinned. She really did have the palate of a twelve-year-old, something she knew she needed to change a little bit. But stuff like bacon was so good. Broccoli? Not so much. "If you've got blueberries, I could eat some."

He glanced over his shoulder at her, lifting an eyebrow. "Fruit? Really? Have the pod people finally taken over?"

"Ha, ha. I'm trying to be more adult."

"You're in luck then, because we've got some. And after breakfast I've got something to give you."

"You gave me plenty last night." Boy, did he ever. More than once, and she was walking on cloud nine now because of it.

He snickered as he slid the sizzling pan off the burner onto a cold one. "Not like that. I got you a Christmas present, and I know it's only Christmas Eve, but..." He shrugged. "I want to give it to you now."

"I didn't bring my gift for you." It was still at home in her bedroom, wrapped up. She just hadn't thought to bring it because things had been so rushed.

"I don't care about that. I just want to give yours to you."

She smiled at him and took a bite of bacon. "Then I will graciously accept your gift."

He ended up making a couple pancakes for them as well, and she had to smile. He really was great in the kitchen. And there was something about eating home-cooked food instead of takeout that she really liked. But truly, the fact that Logan was the one cooking for her was incredibly sweet, and she was trying to wrap her mind around the fact that this could be something real. Not just sex.

After they finished breakfast, she washed the dishes—even though he tried to take over. She figured it was only fair since he'd cooked breakfast. But before she'd even finished drying their plates he was dragging her to the living room. Sure enough a little box was sitting prettily underneath the tree. For a moment her throat tightened with emotion that he'd thought to bring this.

He tugged her down in front of the tree and fireplace and set it into her lap. "Open it."

She looked at the small rectangular box wrapped perfectly with silver-and-green wrapping paper and topped with a bundle of curling silver ribbon. It was very clearly professionally wrapped. "It's so pretty I almost don't want to open it."

"Are you one of those people who unwrap presents slowly?"

"Of course. And I usually save the wrapping paper." She worked in the public school system and was thrifty by nature; she recycled anything she could.

"I guess that's where we definitely differ."

She slid her fingernail under the tape on the back of the gift. "Somehow I'm not surprised. I bet you and your brother were tiny terrors when you were little on Christmas Day."

"We definitely were. It was a massacre of shredded wrapping paper and bags all over our living room floor."

Her heart skipped a beat as she slid the wrapping paper off and looked at the red box inside. It was definitely a jewelry box because she recognized the local jeweler's name etched in gold on the top. "What is this?" she whispered.

He simply grinned.

When she opened it, her eyes widened at the sight of the beautiful, glittering diamond and topaz tennis bracelet. "Logan, this is incredible. It's beautiful. And…" It was waaaaay too much. She'd seen this once when they'd been out on a Sunday doing brunch and window shopping, and mentioned how beautiful it was. Not in a million years had she ever thought he would get her something like this. *Ever.*

"I can read that look in your eyes. Don't say it's too much. Nothing is too much for you." Without waiting for a response, he slid it out of the box and clasped it around her wrist.

She stared at it, then at him. "Thank you," she said quietly. It still was too much but it was gorgeous and she loved it. Still… "I'm almost afraid to wear it. It's so pretty." And the truth was, she was afraid to accept all of this goodness, all this wonderfulness from Logan. She'd always thought that if something seemed too good to be true, then it very likely was. Which was bullshit where he was concerned. She knew that. But...it was hard to remind herself of that, to actually believe it. And right now she was swimming in too many emotions. This gift clearly meant something. He wouldn't buy her something like this unless he was serious.

"The clasp is sturdy. Trust me. I had them check it and everything."

"You're wonderful and this is the best Christmas present I've ever gotten. Thank you." She leaned forward and cupped his cheeks, pressing her mouth to his in a soft exploration.

Even though she was still scared of getting her heart broken, she was in this thing with him. She was giving them a chance. She wanted to see if they had a chance at something real, and he'd been so damn honest with her right from the start. He'd told her what he wanted from her and she was going to put her heart on the line with him.

Almost instantly, he deepened the kiss and she leaned into it, shifting forward until she straddled him, his covered erection rubbing against her core.

"Damn it," he muttered as he pulled back from her. "I've got to grab condoms out of the truck. We ran out last night."

She groaned too, not wanting to be separated from him, not wanting to wait a second longer, but she slid off him. "Well hurry up and grab them. When you get back you can fuck me while I'm in nothing but this bracelet." She lifted her wrist and jangled it slightly.

His eyes heated immediately as he jumped to his feet and adjusted himself. "I'll be fast."

As he hurried toward the foyer, she turned the fireplace off because it was getting too hot—Logan made her hot enough, thank you very much.

As Grace stretched out on the pile of blankets, she debated if she should strip now or let him undress her. Hmmm... She jolted upright, all her muscles tensing as she heard gunshots.

Pop. Pop.

Heart in her throat, she jumped to her feet. Logan!

She raced for the front of the house, stumbling in the foyer when she heard it again. *Pop. Pop.* Oh God, Logan!

Before she could move, the door flew open and Logan barreled through, a weapon in hand as he slammed the door and locked it. "We've gotta go." He raced down the hallway, grabbing her by the hand. "Shoes and pants on now," he ordered as he grabbed a backpack from the closet, then grabbed his own shoes.

Fear spurred her into action. Moving quickly, she tugged on a pair of yoga pants and hurriedly slid on her sneakers.

"Only one shooter that I can tell. He's slashed my tires and he's jammed the electronics because I can't get a call out." Logan's words were clipped as they hurried back down the hall.

The window in one of the front rooms exploded. She bit back a scream as he motioned toward the living room. Her legs were moving but she felt as if she was operating on autopilot.

"We're heading out the back door. We can disappear into the underbrush. We're taking a chance but it's better than being sitting ducks in here when I don't know what kind of weapons he has."

She simply nodded, shoving back the raw fear bubbling up inside her. Whatever Logan thought was best she was going to go with. She wasn't trained for any of this, but she could certainly follow instructions. And run.

Her heart beat wildly in her chest as he slid his pistol out and carefully opened the back door.

Another gunshot sounded from somewhere near the front. She winced, sweat building at the base of her spine.

Logan, who seemed insanely calm about all this, held his hand up and pointed which direction they should go. He stepped out first, then, when it was clear, ordered her to go ahead of him so he could watch her back.

Throat tight, she did as he said, racing across the small backyard to a wide-open stretch of rocks and gravel beyond it. Since they'd walked the path around the property yesterday, she was somewhat familiar with the area but she hoped Logan knew where they were going.

Gravel shot up around them. She let out a scream.

"Keep running!" Logan shouted as he paused and turned, returned fire.

Her entire body shook at the blast of the gunfire. It was so much louder and scarier than in the movies, and absolutely terrifying. But she kept going, knowing that getting to cover was the only way to survive this.

Her legs strained as she raced for the entrance to the walking path. As she sucked in air, she vowed to take up running after this. Or to at least exercise more.

Pop. Pop. Logan shot again.

"I bought us a few minutes," Logan said as he moved up behind her onto the rocky pathway.

They were surrounded by overgrown trees and foliage, thankfully giving them some concealment.

"Where are we going?" she whispered, avoiding the urge to turn around.

Logan had her back so she knew he would keep them safe. And if he fell... *No way.* She wouldn't think like that. They had to get away. Both of them.

"There's a neighborhood about two miles from here. We can make it on foot as long as we keep distance between us and the shooter. Once we get to the end of one of these walking paths, it connects to a main road. From there, we'll be able to make it to the neighborhood."

She nodded instead of responding verbally in an attempt to conserve energy as they continued sprinting over the underbrush. A branch slapped her in the face but she ignored it. Her lungs burned as she jumped over a protruding rock. She didn't care. Her brain was telling her to run, run, run. Then hide.

And stay alive.

She had so many questions, like how the hell had someone found them?

But now was definitely not the time to ask. They just needed to get to safety. She'd left all her stuff back there and she knew he'd left most of his so she hoped he had extra ammo in his backpack. "Can you see him?" She jumped over another rock, her breathing harsh.

"Nope. Take a left up here," he said quietly as they reached a fork in the dusty path.

She didn't pause, simply veered left and continued running. They had enough concealment right now but she was terrified he would catch up with them.

Her breath sawed in and out, the brown and green foliage flying past her in a blur. She felt as if she was in a tunnel, the worst videogame ever, as her sneakers pounded against the rocky path. Her muscles ached and she couldn't stop trembling but no way in hell was she stopping.

"We might have lost him," Logan murmured as they continued running. "But keep going."

She sure hoped so.

A shot rent the air and she stumbled.

Logan caught her by the shoulder. "He's blindly shooting," he said before she could panic.

She looked over her shoulder at him and he held a finger to his lips.

She nodded and turned around to face forward again, continuing onward. Every movement, every huff of breath felt overpronounced, as if the shooter would jump out of the brush at any moment because he'd heard their movements.

When she noticed the underbrush thinning ahead, her heart leapt. They must be near the main road Logan had mentioned. But just as quickly, more fear settled in her gut. If their cover was getting thinner, they were easier targets.

"Keep going," Logan whispered.

On a burst of speed, she sprinted forward. She had no doubt that Logan had been keeping pace with her because the man was in incredible shape. He could probably run twice as fast as her but he was sticking with her to protect her.

As they reached the end of the path there was a wide-open stretch of asphalt just as he'd said.

She felt incredibly exposed and vulnerable in that moment. But logically she knew there was no way the shooter could have gotten ahead of them. Unless...he'd figured out a shortcut.

The fear was back, shoving up and threatening to choke her. She kept imagining him jumping from the bushes, gun in hand, and shooting them down.

Logan pointed to the right and they started running once again, side by side this time, their sneakers beating against the road with little thumps. He still had his gun in hand and was barely out of breath—unlike Grace, who felt like she was about to die at any moment. Her lungs burned and all her muscles strained.

Fear settled deep inside her and she imagined this nameless, faceless shooter taking aim at them, hitting them in the back while she and Logan were unable to stop a thing. When she saw a turnoff to a neighborhood up ahead, joy burst inside her like fireworks.

They were so close.

But instead of turning into the neighborhood's main entrance, Logan took her arm and directed her off the main road and to the back wall that lined part of the neighborhood.

"We're going to jump over the wall." He turned around, scanning the road for any signs of the shooter.

"What if someone's home?"

"I don't care. We're hiding now." Bending down in front of her, he linked his fingers together.

Immediately she put her foot in his cupped hands. In one quick movement, he hoisted her up. Clutching at the cold stone, she crawled over the wall, and basically rolled into a bunch of bushes.

She winced at the impact, but stayed quiet as Logan climbed over the wall with incredible ease. He slid down next to her in a sleek, skilled move and pulled out his phone.

"It's finally working." Relief was clear in those few words.

Her heart was still pounding erratically but they'd found a place to hide at least. And Logan still had a weapon to protect them.

As Logan called his brother and started filling Roman in on what had happened, she peered through the bushes into the backyard, glad they were hidden by all the palm trees and giant cacti. There were even more cacti underneath a couple of the windows and it looked as if blinds were drawn on them so hopefully no one had seen them dive into the backyard. If they had, the owners had probably called the police, but that was more than okay with Grace.

After a few minutes, Logan slid his phone into his back pocket. "Roman is with Vadim and he's tracking us using my phone. They're on the way."

"Mine's still back at the house," she muttered. She'd run out of there without even a bra on and everything was finally catching up to her. They still weren't out of danger as it was. Just hiding from it. "Do you know how he found us? Did you see him?" She kept her voice low, not wanting it to carry on the wind.

"No and no." He tightened his jaw and reached for her, pulling her close. "This place is quiet so we'll just stay here until Roman calls me. It might be a while, since they're in the city."

"Okay." As long as help came. Instead of crouching, she sat fully down, collapsing and pressing her back against the wall. Dragging in breaths, she leaned her head on Logan's shoulder. The cold wrapped around her, chilling her to the bone, but she didn't care.

They were alive. For now.

She just hoped help arrived soon.

CHAPTER 25

Grace gratefully took the blanket Logan wrapped around her shoulders as they sat on the couch in the plush hotel room at the Serafina. Roman and Vadim had picked them up hours ago and driven them back to Vegas, but she was still so chilled. So afraid. No matter that the room was warm, she couldn't get rid of the chill that seemed to have overtaken her entire body.

Detective Hurley was here to talk to them, though she knew there was a team of police dealing with the mess in the house they'd stayed at. At least someone had brought all their stuff to the casino, though it was all with security at this point.

Wyatt Christiansen had also arrived to talk to them, which surprised her. She'd seen him on the news with his wife, and while she vaguely knew Iris, Wyatt was so intimidating and a bit larger than life in person. Iris was too, but she always had a smile for Grace and was much more approachable.

"At this point I think we might want to put you guys into protective custody," Detective Hurley said carefully as he shifted in his seat.

"No." Wyatt spoke before Logan or Grace could respond.

The detective raised an eyebrow as he turned to look at Wyatt, who was standing next to the huge wall of windows, all of Vegas behind him as if it was his domain. Which it might as well be, for how much power he wielded in the city. She wondered if his position in the room was some sort of power play because he and the detective had been eyeing each other warily.

"Excuse me?" the detective said.

"No. I can keep them safer than you guys can. No offense." Wyatt lifted his shoulders.

The detective cleared his throat. "Look—"

"Whatever you're going to say, the answer is still no. They don't have to go into protective custody with you and they're not going to. I should have done this before but you guys didn't think the threat was that serious." He looked at Logan and then Grace, his expression softening a fraction. "I'm sorry this happened at all. I should have just put you guys up somewhere instead of—"

"This is no one's fault," Logan said, tightening his fingers around Grace's. "We should have been safe at my friend's place."

Detective Hurley stood, clearly knowing he was beat. "All right, then. When we find out how he tracked you, we'll be in touch," he said, his expression grim.

Grace simply nodded and waited as Wyatt walked the detective to the door, talking quietly.

She leaned into Logan, needing his warmth. Even after what they'd been through earlier today, she still felt safe with him. Or maybe because of seeing him in action. His quick thinking, getting them out of the house within moments, had given them a much better chance of surviving. She didn't even want to think about what might have happened if they hadn't gotten out of there.

"I've got a few options for you guys," Wyatt said as he strode back into the room. "All of them here at the casino. I've got multiple open suites available, and there won't be any cleaning services. No food delivery that isn't authorized will be allowed into the room. It'll be a total lockdown and only people I personally approve will be allowed inside the suite."

"Thank you," Logan said, squeezing Grace's hand.

"I really am sorry that it escalated to this," Wyatt said. "I should have insisted on this before." There was a hint of self-recrimination in his expression.

Logan shook his head. "Look, no one expected this, least of all *me*. We should have been fine where we were. I'm not blaming anyone for anything other than the asshole gunning for us."

"I didn't want to say this in front of Hurley, but Vadim discovered that you guys were tracked using Grace's phone," Wyatt said, looking at her.

"How? It's never been out of my possession." Even at school she locked it in her desk. And since she hadn't even been at work since all this started, it had been in her purse or pocket. She even used it as an alarm clock, so it was often on her nightstand in the evenings as well.

"Someone hacked your phone using your email account. Vadim says it looks like you clicked on something, a link from an ad, and someone infiltrated your phone's location tracking that way."

She wrapped her arms around herself. That sounded horrifying. "How easy is it for someone to do that?"

"Apparently it's *not* easy. And whoever did it tracked you in a way that makes it impossible for Vadim to track back to them."

And it just got even worse. "So...why aren't we telling the police?"

"It doesn't really matter how you were found. It just matters that we find whoever did this." There was a definite bite of anger to the man's words.

She figured they weren't telling the cops because Vadim had illegally done some stuff. She didn't care what he'd done to get the information. She was just glad they were okay and had at least figured out how they'd been tracked.

"Has Vadim secured her phone?" Logan asked.

"Yes. He's got it and all your stuff up in security. I'll have it all brought to you when we figure out where you're staying. I've got a couple suites ready, so unless you have a preference for views, I recommend the Monroe suite. It's bigger than the others and has been empty for a couple weeks. You can monitor who comes in and out easily. I'm going to put security on the door as well. Only people I trust."

Logan stood again. "Thank you for this. But my friend's house just got shot up. I need to make sure—"

"I've already taken care of it," Wyatt said, holding up a hand. "The forensics team has already done what they need to do. Technically it's still a crime scene but Hurley is letting us put the house back together. The windows will be repaired and the glass cleaned up. And I've had your rental truck towed. If you need a vehicle, you can take one of the casino vehicles. You two don't need to worry about any of that now."

"Okay. And thank you. Just keep me updated. I want to tell him what happened, but reassure him that everything is fine with his place when I do."

Grace knew Logan felt bad about what had happened, but it wasn't his fault. Reaching out, she took his hand in hers, squeezing it once. It didn't remotely feel like Christmas Eve but she was glad she was with him.

He glanced down at her, still standing, and smiled.

"I will," Wyatt said. "But don't worry about that stuff. Just worry about your lady." Wyatt nodded once at her and left.

Still holding Logan's hand, she sank back against the soft buttercream-tufted couch, pulling him down with her. "This is all so surreal. I don't even have a bra on," she muttered. They'd run out of there so fast.

Logan quickly gathered her into his arms. "I'm so sorry about all of this," he said as she buried her face against his chest. The grip of his arms around her was safe, familiar. Wonderful.

"I think everyone needs to stop with apologies." She leaned back to look at him. "I know I said I don't think Kevin is behind this, and I still *don't*. But...he is good with computers." And it was something Logan and probably Vadim needed to know. She figured the cops already did since they were looking for him.

Logan nodded once as if he already knew that.

Closing her eyes, she laid her cheek against his chest again and decided to block out the rest of the world for a long moment. "Do you think we can order room service in that suite he's putting us up in?"

His grip around her tightened. "I'm pretty sure we can order whatever we want, including a bottle of his best wine. Wyatt doesn't half-ass things."

Despite the turmoil congealed inside her, she smiled. "Logan..." She wasn't sure what she was going to say but her throat suddenly wouldn't work. Tears pushed against her eyelids, spilling over in a giant wave. *Oh God, noooo.* She didn't want to have a breakdown. Had thought she was keeping it together pretty well.

He cursed softly before rubbing a hand up and down her spine as she started full-on crying. "Just get it out."

She tried to fight it but it was useless. The more she tried to fight it, the faster the tears flowed. The events of the day cascaded down on her like a rockslide. She'd thought she'd been handling everything so well but today had pushed her over the edge. Being shot at like that, having someone hunting them down—she'd never experienced or imagined a terror like that before.

In that moment, she could only imagine how Logan had served in the Marines, how he'd dealt with a whole lot worse than today. It blew her mind and made her especially aware of her own mortality. And on that thought, she wrapped her arms tighter around him, wishing she could find the right words, but she was mentally tapped out.

Absolutely and utterly done. She was just glad Logan was here to hold her.

To keep her safe.

***

Logan stepped out of the huge bedroom of the suite they'd been put in to find Grace stretched out on one of the soft white chaise lounges. She'd moved it from the living room where it faced an oversized television so that it was now facing out the window overlooking the city.

She had a plush white robe belted loosely around her. Her toned legs were stretched out in front of her, and she had a glass of champagne in her hand.

"You look sexy as fuck," he murmured, dropping onto the other chair she must have moved as well.

As he sank down into the plush seat, she smiled. "I figure I'm never going to have a chance to stay in a place like this so I'm taking advantage. Trying to make lemonade from lemons and all that."

"Why won't you get that chance?"

She lifted an eyebrow. "I work for the public school system. A night here is like...probably a couple months' paychecks. Maybe more."

"You're probably not too far off the mark." Wyatt had put them in one of the penthouse suites, and while Logan wasn't sure how much this place cost he knew it was pricey and probably half a year's salary for her. It was where the Serafina put their high rollers. Leaning over, he grabbed the bottle of champagne—which was almost empty—from the bronze ice bucket and poured himself a glass.

"This is such an Instagram moment," she said, giggling, and he was glad the champagne had loosened her up and hopefully eased some of her tension.

He'd hated that she'd been crying, though he understood why. But it had made him feel helpless because there'd been nothing to do to stop her tears. Nothing other than stopping the bastard after them. "Are you on Instagram?"

"Yep. It's one of my only social media accounts and I love it. I find out all sorts of cool things that teachers and counselors around the country and world are doing. And of course I get unlimited access to cute dog pictures."

He laughed lightly. He knew she was thinking about adopting a rescue and was hoping to do so once summer started. "Have you ever thought about teaching instead of being a guidance counselor?"

She nodded. "Yes. I go back and forth on whether it would be right for me, because I love what I do."

He reached out with his free hand and linked his fingers through hers as he looked out at the city in front of them. "You'd make a good teacher." She was so kind and giving.

"Thanks." She sighed almost happily and took a sip of her drink.

"You seem like you're doing a little better." For that he was grateful.

"I am. Thanks for letting me cry it out on you earlier. I feel like I should be embarrassed."

He tightened his fingers in hers. "No, you shouldn't. And I'm surprised it didn't come out earlier, to be honest."

She took a sip of her champagne and laid her head back against the lounge chair. That was when he noticed she was wearing the bracelet he'd given her. "The reality of it all sort of crashed over me all at once. It's hard to grasp that someone wants us, or one of us, dead."

"I know." He tightened his fingers in hers again as he watched her.

She looked so incredible just lying there, her robe loose around her, split up the middle to reveal her bare, sexy legs. Legs he'd had draped over his shoulders more than once. *Fuuuck.* His cock hardened just thinking about that.

Setting his glass down on a little side table, he moved to her chair and sat on the end of it. This woman completely owned him, even if she didn't realize it.

She gave him a lethargic, relaxed look. "What's up?"

Instead of answering, he shifted so that he was kneeling at the end of the lounge and slowly started spreading her robe all the way open.

Setting down her glass, she hitched in a breath as she watched him—and made no attempt to stop him.

"You just sit back and relax," he murmured. *Hell yeah.* He just wanted her to enjoy herself. Those tears from earlier had destroyed him.

Her cheeks turned pink as he reached for the tie on her robe and tugged. It was already so loosely belted, and once it was untied it completely opened to reveal his fantasy.

She had nothing on underneath—nothing on at all except the robe and her new bracelet. Her nipples were already hard, her chest rising and falling a little erratically as the robe slid to her sides. It was still technically on her, but showing all the best parts. He was so gone for her.

Reaching between her legs, he slid a finger along her folds. Slowly he started teasing her, barely dipping his finger inside her while keeping his gaze on her face.

She was so expressive, hitching in a breath each time he grazed her clit. He knew how to tease her, loved doing it. But he couldn't wait any longer to taste her.

His self-control was shot where she was concerned. Bending down, he began teasing her in earnest, flicking his tongue against her slick folds, tasting, devouring. She was everything to him and if he could make her forget about the bullshit they were dealing with, for even a little bit, he was going to.

Almost immediately she slid her fingers through his hair and clutched at him, holding tight. "Logan." She moaned it out like a soft prayer.

He loved hearing his name on her lips. Anytime, *all* the time. Hell, he craved it.

Things had definitely shifted between them and he was so damn happy. They might have only been on one date that ended badly, but she was opening up to him, not pushing him away. The fact that she'd accepted his Christmas present meant everything. The walls that had been between them were finally down. He never would have been able to give her the bracelet before. But he clearly saw the way she looked at him now, with more than just lust and hunger.

He continued teasing her, focusing on her clit, giving her all the pressure she needed. He wanted to take the edge off for her, wanted her to find release so she could relax even more. His cock was heavy between his legs but that was too damn bad for him. He'd find release later. Hopefully with her.

She rolled her hips against his face and he groaned against her. God, he loved her taste. Everything about her was addicting.

He slid two fingers inside her, curling them back and stroking against her inner walls as he sucked on her clit.

And that set her off. Taking him by surprise, she jerked against him, sucking in a breath as her climax started to build. So he kept going, kept teasing with his fingers and mouth until she completely fell over the edge into a long, drawn out release.

Finally she gripped his head, her breathing harsh. "Enough."

"It's never enough," he murmured as he crawled up her body, capturing her mouth with his, letting her taste herself.

She wrapped her arms and legs around him. "You're insatiable," she murmured against his mouth.

For her? Yeah, he definitely was. He was never going to get enough of her. Wrapping his own arms around her, he lifted her up. It was definitely time to make use of the giant bed in the other room. And he wanted space for what he had planned for her.

She giggled lightly as he scooped her up and headed in that direction.

In that moment, he was so damn tempted to tell her that he loved her. But...it was too soon. He wasn't walking away from her, from a relationship, but he wanted to make sure she was ready to hear the words from him before he dropped the L bomb on her. They'd come so far and he wasn't going to screw this up.

CHAPTER 26

Logan sat up at the sound of his phone ringing because he recognized the ring tone as Roman's. Didn't matter that it was a few hours to sunrise, he was fully awake now as he grabbed the phone.

Grace rolled over, tangled in the sheets, and looked at him sleepily. She mumbled something before closing her eyes so he kissed her on the forehead and snagged his phone.

"Yeah?" he answered softly, striding from the huge bedroom without bothering with clothing.

"I'm on my way up. The cops have a lead on Brister. Found him holed up in Vegas."

He froze for all of a millisecond, then strode right back toward the bedroom and started tugging on his discarded clothing. "You're sure?"

"Vadim is definitely sure. They're going to be making a move on him soon. They got a tip that he's in a motel nearby."

"Hurley will lose his shit if we show up."

"Do you care?"

He snorted. Nope. But... "I'm not leaving Grace unprotected."

"I know. Even though there are two guys on the door I'm bringing a replacement with me who will stay in the living room. She won't be alone for a second."

He breathed out a sigh of relief. He trusted his brother without reservation. "See you in a few."

By now Grace was already sitting up in bed, tucking the sheet neatly around her perfect breasts.

"You should never cover those up," he murmured as he grabbed a pair of sneakers from the floor.

"No way. Don't try to distract me. What's going on?"

"They have a hit on Brister in the city."

She blinked. "Wait...he's here? Who found him?"

"The cops. Roman and I are just going to..." He cleared his throat. "We're going to head down there and make sure they actually bring Brister in. That's all." He needed to see with his own eyes that the man was taken in.

She sighed and for a moment looked like she wanted to argue with him. "Just don't get in trouble with the cops. I'll post your bail, but I'd rather not." Her tone was dry, but he could see a hint of worry in her dark eyes.

"I won't. I swear, I'm not going armed or anything. I just want to make sure he gets arrested. We'll be sitting across the street." *Maybe.*

She nodded and let the sheet fall as she got out of bed.

He groaned and pulled her into a hug, savoring the feel of her soft curves against his body and wishing he could get right back in bed with her. "You're going to have to get dressed. Roman's bringing someone with him to keep an eye on you."

She tightened her grip around him. "I thought there were guards outside."

"There are, but I want someone in the room as well."

"I would say it seems like overkill but my feet and leg muscles are still sore from running through the desert, so okay."

His thoughts exactly. He kissed her briefly and pulled back at the sound of a knock coming from the other room. "Hey, before I leave...Merry Christmas." Hell, he couldn't believe it was Christmas Day. Sure didn't feel like it.

She blinked once then smiled. "Merry Christmas."

"I'll be back soon and we'll celebrate."

"Okay. Just shut the bedroom door on your way out. I'm going to shower first but I'll be out later."

He pulled her into a hug one more time, then sighed at the sound of his brother pounding on the door again.

The security guys had an access key but Roman was probably not using it in case they were in here naked. Sighing, he shut the bedroom door behind him and hurried to the main door. Through the peephole he saw Roman, Vadim and another guy. Logan yanked the door open. It was four in the morning now and he needed coffee.

As soon as he tugged it fully open, he grinned when Roman held out a to-go cup of coffee for him. His twin certainly knew him. His grin faded as his gaze landed on the security guy named Jordan standing there. Jordan was…well, good-looking was an understatement. He'd heard more than one woman, and some men, comment on the guy's looks. Because yeah, he looked like a model—had apparently been one as a teenager. Bronze skin, bright green eyes, sharp cheekbones that Logan was annoyed as shit he was even noticing. He frowned at the guy.

"Jordan's going to stay in the room," Vadim said, the barest hint of a smile tugging at his mouth.

He simply nodded and stepped back. "She's in the bedroom. Don't bother her in there. She'll come out when she's ready and she might go back to sleep, so keep it down."

"Yeah, I know. Not my first security gig," Jordan murmured, frowning at Logan in annoyance. "I'll be out in the living room. Got my phone on me if anyone needs me, and I've worked with these guys before," he said, motioning to the two men standing guard outside.

Logan just grunted, and as they left, Vadim actually snickered.

"What?" Logan growled.

Vadim shrugged. "Nothing."

"Did you pick that handsome bastard intentionally?" Because Jordan truly was good-looking in a way even Logan could recognize. He wasn't insecure exactly, but...damn. He was acting like a jackass. He trusted Grace and he liked Jordan.

"That's what you get for hitting on Angel."

"Dude," he said as he pressed the elevator button. "That was *years* ago. And I wasn't actually hitting on her anyway. I was just screwing with you."

Vadim shot him a dark look. "My memory is long and I am not a forgiving man."

"Come on, children." Roman's tone was dry as he ushered both of them into the elevator. "Let's talk specifics. We're definitely staying out of the way of the police, but when we get close to the motel, I'm at least texting Hurley to let him know we're nearby."

"He's going to be so pissed that we're showing up for this." Not that Logan cared.

Roman simply shrugged as they reached the bottom floor. "It's not like we're going to get in the way. We'll be across the street and that's not breaking the law."

"How we found out about this is illegal," Vadim murmured, grinning in an uncharacteristic way. "If we get arrested, we can just contact Wyatt's attorney."

"You're in an exceptionally good mood this morning," Logan muttered to Vadim. He sure wasn't, because he had to leave Grace behind—and think about her spending time with that handsome bastard instead of him.

"Indeed I am." Vadim didn't expand, just gave Logan a smug look. Which could have meant any number of things.

Logan sighed. "I'm sorry I messed with you about Angel. I...didn't understand what it was like to fall for someone back then. I was just having fun, but it was messed up of me."

Vadim looked surprised as they hurried toward the parking garage. "You're really into Grace?"

He nodded as they reached Roman's truck. "She's it for me." He wasn't going to say that he loved her because he hadn't told her yet. But yeah, he knew how he felt. It was way too soon to tell her, however. She was too damn skittish as it was.

"I almost feel a little bad about specifically requesting Jordan for this detail." Vadim paused before opening the door. "Almost."

Rolling his eyes, Logan jumped into the passenger side and slid his seat belt on. "Let's get the hell out of here."

It took them a solid ten minutes to get to the motel but instead of parking there, where they clearly saw a handful of black-and-whites, Roman parked across the street at a Denny's with a neon sign proclaiming it was open twenty-four hours.

"Here." From the backseat Vadim handed Logan a pair of binoculars.

Surprised, he grabbed them. "This is military-grade stuff." Not that he would expect Vadim to have shit equipment, but still, towing around heavy duty binos was out of the ordinary.

"I like to be prepared."

Apparently. Holding them up to his eyes, he zoomed in a bit until the focus cleared and he could see six men in SWAT gear approaching a second-story door.

Three men were on either side of the door and using hand signals he recognized even though he'd never been in law enforcement. "They're heading in now."

He watched as they moved like a well-oiled machine, the front man kicking the door in, weapon up, and then the others filing inside in a perfect formation.

Less than five minutes later, the lead guy came outside with... "It's him. It's Brister. And holy shit, he looks drunk." Thanks to the clarity of the binoculars, Logan could see the man's bloodshot eyes as they hauled him out in handcuffs. The officer in tactical gear was smoothly walking him down the stairs, even helping him stay upright as he would have tumbled down the last couple stairs without support.

"Look alive," his brother murmured.

"What?"

"Put the binoculars down."

He did as his brother said and winced when he saw Hurley striding across the street toward them, his expression dark. *Damn it.*

Logan slid the binoculars back to Vadim, then opened the door and got out. To his surprise Roman and Vadim stepped out as well.

"I want to ask how you knew this was going down," Detective Hurley said as he shot Vadim a dark look. "But I already know the answer. You guys shouldn't be here. *You* especially shouldn't be here." Now his laser-like focus was on Logan.

"I'm just a patron of fine dining."

The detective snorted and glanced over his shoulder.

Brister, handcuffed and cursing up a storm, was being led to a waiting black-and-white. Even through his drunken haze he must have somehow recognized Logan across the street because he started shouting wildly.

"You ruined my life!" Or at least that was what it sounded like before he got shoved into the back of the car and the door slammed shut.

"Glad you found him," Logan said, focusing on Hurley now.

"He's in a whole lot of trouble. But...we still need a confession. We can't prove he was behind anything. Not specifically. There's been no evidence so far and he's drunk as hell. We've got him for a bit until they drag him back to Montana if we can't nail him for something in Vegas."

"Check his phone," Logan said. "There's a possibility he tracked Grace using some kind of technology."

"Some kind of technology?"

"That's just a guess."

Hurley's gaze narrowed slightly. "Well you guys won't have to worry about Grace's ex-fiancé anymore either."

Logan lifted his eyebrows.

"He's back in California and has been for the last thirty-six hours apparently. It looks like he drove instead of flying. I confirmed with his wife that he was there. Now you all need to get out of here. You saw what you came to see. I don't want anything screwing up this arrest, got it?"

Logan nodded because he did get it. "I'm sorry. Thank you. And Merry Christmas." He held out a hand and was glad the detective shook it, murmuring back a Merry Christmas to him.

He didn't want to get on Hurley's bad side and the guy was being fairly decent, considering they'd all shown up unannounced to a SWAT operation on

Christmas Day. It didn't matter that they'd been across the street because clearly it wasn't a coincidence that they were here. *With binoculars.*

"You know anything about Grace's ex?" Logan asked as soon as they were back in Roman's truck.

"Yeah," Vadim said. "I just got a hit on him before we picked you up. He headed back home via a private plane, not a car as Hurley seems to think. He must have hit up a wealthy acquaintance. I also might have hacked his email and sent some very interesting photos to his wife. He's back home right now but he's certainly going to be hating life for a while. His wife has got some nice pictures for her divorce attorney if she needs them."

Logan turned around in surprise. "Nice work."

Vadim gave him a dark smile. "The guy's an asshole. And I like Grace. I consider myself doing karma's work." He shrugged.

"Grace is somehow under the impression that you are a mushy teddy bear. Her words, not mine."

To his surprise Vadim actually grinned. "Angel thinks the same thing about me."

Logan shook his head and turned back around. Vadim was a scary-ass bastard Logan never wanted to be on the bad side of. "How bad were the pictures?"

"They involved him and a couple strippers at once. That's what he gets for saving the images. Dumbass. Whatever he told his wife he was doing in Vegas, I don't think it was that." He let out a short laugh. "I also hacked his wife's email and she's already been in contact with a couple lawyers. I think she'll come out on the other side okay."

"You really are a softy," Logan said laughingly.

"Yeah, yeah, just don't let it get out."

"Hey, thanks for coming out on Christmas. I really do appreciate it."

Vadim just shrugged. "Angel is understanding. And I'll be back in time for presents."

"You gonna thank me too?" Roman muttered. "Your twin?"

Logan just punched him in the arm and picked up his phone. He quickly texted Grace, telling her about her ex, but not *all* the details. Just that Kevin was in California, and that Brister had been arrested. They would both be able to sleep easier tonight at least, and soon they'd be able to head home. Talk about a good Christmas present.

Logan just hoped that Hurley was able to get a confession out of Brister. Either way the man should be sent back to Montana soon, because there was a warrant out for his arrest. And Logan wanted the guy out of the state so he wouldn't be tempted to hunt Brister down and beat the shit out of him. Maybe worse.

Brister had come after him and his woman, had clearly wanted to kill them. Logan was feeling protective, possessive and a little murderous right now. Grace was everything to him. He wouldn't let anyone try to take her from him.

CHAPTER 27

"You can leave now," Logan said as he stepped into the living room of the hotel suite to find Grace and Jordan sitting on opposite couches talking pleasantly to each other.

"Everything good?" Jordan asked as he stood, as if at attention.

Grace gave Logan a strange look as he nodded. "Yep, we're good to go." He forced himself to *not* act like a jackass. The guy was just doing his job—protecting Grace. And Logan was grateful. Wasn't the man's fault that Logan was feeling possessive and protective. He'd never even experienced this before, never thought he could be this weirdly jealous. "Thank you for coming here on such short notice."

Jordan shook his hand once, then clapped him on the shoulder. "Of course, no problem. It was nice meeting you, Grace. Hopefully I'll see you around."

"You too. Thank you for keeping me company." She was already standing as well and smiling at the other man as Jordan started to head out.

And Logan had the irrational urge to want to keep all her smiles only for him. He knew it was absolutely ridiculous but he couldn't squash the thought.

"So what happened?" Grace was in front of him, wrapping her arms around him in a tight embrace as the door shut behind Jordan.

Just like that, his irrational jealousy over absolutely nothing melted away and he wrapped his arms around her, glad to have her close again. "SWAT team busted into his room and arrested him." He'd told her that Brister had been arrested, but hadn't given specific details of his takedown. "It was all very quick and professional. They hauled him out in cuffs and that was that."

Her eyes widened. "Wow. I can't believe he's really in Vegas. That he really came after us over his own garbage."

"I don't have any more details but I can safely say that he is in custody and they're going to be questioning him. I'm sure once they get what they need he'll end up being extradited back to Montana. Or maybe they'll just keep him here and book him if they end up getting priority. I'm really not sure how that works and I don't actually care. But Detective Hurley told me he'd keep us updated."

"So are we good to go home?" Her eyes lit up and he tightened his grip around her.

"Yeah but I think we could probably get a quickie in before we have to leave." *Hell yeah.* He needed more of Grace, right now.

She threw her head back and laughed, and he felt that sound all the way to his core. "We better hurry then, because I'm pretty sure this room is a few thousand a night."

"That's probably on the low end," he murmured, his gaze falling to her mouth. "And I'm kidding about the quickie. Wyatt won't care if we stay the rest of the day."

Her eyes went heavy-lidded. "Then I'm in. Merry Christmas to me," she murmured.

"Merry Christmas to me too." He might hate what had thrown them together, but he loved that he was spending Christmas morning with her.

His cock hardened at the feel of her in his arms, but before he kissed her, before they stopped talking altogether for a while, he said, "Have dinner with me and my parents tonight?"

She blinked. "Of course. Although…are you sure? Because I'm sure your parents want to spend time with you."

"They want to see both of us, to have a late Christmas dinner with me and you. Roman told me on the way back here to plan on a very casual dinner."

"Should I bring anything?"

"Just yourself."

"That sounds like a plan. Though I do have a real present for you."

"Why don't you just give me my present now?" He gave her a wicked grin and she laughed again as she jumped him, wrapping her arms and legs around him.

"This will be your first present, then."

Oh, he would take it, but he wanted more from her. He wanted every Christmas Day from this day forward.

CHAPTER 28

As Grace headed home in her newly fixed car, she was grateful that the auto repair shop had been open today since it was the day after Christmas. She and Logan had ended up staying at the hotel all day, and then Christmas night. Wyatt had told them to just take another night. She felt a little bad that he'd missed Christmas with his family but it had been so nice to simply be with Logan. They'd taken advantage of room service and the giant whirlpool hot tub in the bathroom. It had been heaven.

Now it was back to reality, but she felt good to be driving her own car again, especially since it was free of bullet holes now. Logan had dropped her off and she'd be meeting him in a few hours to do a belated Christmas with his family.

She was still trying to wrap her mind around everything, including the fact that Brister had come down to Vegas with the sole purpose of killing Logan. And clearly he hadn't cared who got in his way. Least of all her, some random woman.

She was still angry that he'd tracked them using her cell phone. It kind of surprised her that he had the technological sense to do it, since he was older and a rancher, but that was what she got for making assumptions. She wouldn't have the first clue about how to track somebody.

It seemed like an eternity and not a month since sleeping with Logan that first time, and then all the insanity of Brister trying to kill them. And...as she pulled up to a stoplight, she realized something disturbing. Quickly, she started doing math in her head and realized that she hadn't had her period for over a month. Wait, no, that couldn't be right.

No way, it couldn't be that long... But yes, she'd had it before Thanksgiving and now it was after Christmas. Ice crept along her veins as reality sank in.

It didn't mean anything. She'd been under a lot of stress, to put it mildly.

Still... When the light turned green, she took a right instead of a left and drove to the nearby CVS. Even though she felt silly grabbing a pregnancy test, she did it anyway.

She and Logan had used condoms. So very many of them. A ridiculous amount, in fact. But sometimes life happened.

She grabbed a bottle of water as well and started chugging it on the way home. By the time she'd made it home, she couldn't ignore the pressure in her bladder and hurried to the bathroom, test in hand.

It didn't matter that she told herself she was making a big deal out of this, that she'd just wasted fifteen dollars. She still had to check.

Just in case.

CHAPTER 29

Grace fought the nausea swelling through her as she knocked on Logan's front door. This was so much different than the last time she'd been here. Even though they were safe from that lunatic Brister, she now had a whole other issue to deal with. One she was going to put off talking about until later.

For a brief second she thought about turning and running away like a coward but the door swung open before she could.

Logan stood there, wonderful Logan with a big smile, and he immediately pulled her into a hug. "I'm glad you're here." He kissed her soundly on the mouth before stepping back and tugging her inside.

Breathless and still nervous, she managed to smile. She'd come by tonight to celebrate Christmas the day after with his family, but she just wanted to curl up under her covers and not come out. She'd said she would be here though, and if she'd canceled, Logan would have worried—and would have likely checked on her. "I'm glad to be here," she said, injecting happiness in her voice even though her mind was a chaotic mess.

He narrowed his gaze slightly. "Grace—"

"Grace!" Taylor came bounding in with a pointed, green-and-red-striped elf hat on. "You've got to try this eggnog!"

The thought of eggnog made her want to puke. Actually, the thought of anything did. Maybe that pregnancy test was a mistake. It had to be, right? They'd used so many damn condoms. She simply couldn't be pregnant. Even though panic swelled, she shoved it down for now. She could get through dinner and then she would handle her emotions at home. And try to process them.

"I would love some hot tea." Maybe that would settle her nerves.

"Yeah, I heard you guys got into the champagne yesterday," Taylor said, pulling her into a tight hug. "I've missed you!"

Despite herself she laughed lightly. "I haven't even been gone that long."

"I know, but I missed talking on the phone, texting, and we had all those plans to go to the movies and do fun classes."

"We'll definitely catch up on those, I promise." She still had a few days before school started back up, and right now all she could think about was seeing her doctor.

Logan curled his arm around her shoulders. "Come on, everyone's waiting on the back patio. They've got a stack of presents for us out there."

"Us?" she asked, looking up at him. God, how was he going to react if this was really happening? They'd only just solidified their relationship. This was something neither of them were ready for.

"Oh yeah, my parents got you presents too."

"I feel a little bad—I didn't get them anything."

"It doesn't matter, trust me. They're just happy we're here."

Even though she was fighting stupid nerves in her belly, she pulled a present out of her purse for him. "I got this for you. It's not a huge deal or anything—"

"Don't do that. Whatever it is, it's amazing." He plucked it from her hand, his eyes searching hers.

She had put a lot of thought into it. "I'm pretty sure you're going to love it."

He started to respond, then they stepped outside onto the patio and he hadn't been kidding. There was a stack of presents on the table and everybody was sitting around the stone fire pit near the pool. Both his parents stood when they saw her and she suddenly found herself enveloped in hugs by everyone, including Roman. The whole thing brought up another swell of emotions and she had to shove them all back again.

"We're so happy you guys are out of the woods. I can only imagine how terrifying that must have been for you," Logan's mom said, dragging Grace toward the chair right next to her.

Logan swooped in before she could sit and sat down instead, tugging her into his lap.

She felt somewhat more settled in his arms, but she didn't like keeping this from him. It was just one test and might not mean anything. It could easily be a mistake—it wasn't like she had any symptoms—but it was all she could focus on even as she responded to Logan's mom that yes, things had been terrifying.

"First I have to open this present from Grace," Logan said, changing the subject and quieting everyone down.

She hated being the center of attention but everyone stared at them as he opened the envelope. When he saw what was inside, his eyes widened.

"You don't have to take me or anything," she murmured. "I just knew you really wanted to go."

He kissed her soundly on the mouth, stealing her breath for a moment. Just like that, the tension melted out of her for a few blissful seconds.

"This is awesome!" Roman said as he grabbed the tickets. "Tickets to *O* by Cirque du Soleil. How did you get front-row seats? This is always sold out."

"One of the teachers I work with. Her husband has an in and he hooked me up."

"Thank you," Logan murmured, kissing her again. "And I'm definitely taking you."

His words warmed her up from the inside out.

"Present time!" Taylor grabbed two bags from the table and handed them to Grace and Logan.

As she opened the presents from his parents, more warmth spread through her even as it mixed with fear. Because if she was really pregnant, it would ruin everything. She and Logan had been building to something wonderful. She loved him. But...this changed everything. It was one thing to be ready for a relationship, but something entirely different to be ready for parenthood. That was...too much.

Even as she tried not to think about it, it seemed that it was all she could think about.

By the time they finished unwrapping presents, she was on the verge of tears, though she was hiding it.

Everyone was so damn wonderful and this gave her a glimpse of what having a great family could be like. Yet she felt absolutely out of place even though she and Logan were actually dating now. They weren't faking anymore, but still, she felt as if she didn't fit in and she knew that was her own issue to deal with.

Combined with the potential pregnancy? She was just emotionally overwhelmed right now, that was all.

She had a damn degree in psychology. She *knew* that was what was going on. But it didn't do anything to ease the racing thoughts in her head. The tension spreading across the back of her skull.

"Thank you guys so much." She tucked a pretty cashmere scarf into one of the gift bags where she was storing the rest of her presents. "This scarf is really beautiful."

"I got that after I met you because I knew it would look beautiful on you," his mom said, beaming at her.

Everyone started talking at once, then Taylor talked about playing some kind of Christmas game.

"I'll be back in a minute," she whispered to Logan and hurried inside.

In the bathroom she splashed cold water on her face and pushed back the tears. "Get it together," she ordered herself. The cold water helped her feel a little better but when she stepped out of the bathroom and nearly ran into Logan, she jerked to a halt.

"What's going on?" he demanded quietly.

"What do you mean?"

"Something's bothering you. I don't think anyone else can tell, but I know you. What's going on? Are you having a hard time dealing with everything?" His expression softened as he watched her.

"Yes, it's just a whole lot." Which was true. To an extent.

His gaze narrowed slightly. "Don't lie to me. We don't lie to each other."

"It's nothing. I don't want to talk about it here." She kept her voice low even though everyone was still outside.

He stepped forward, practically barreling his way into the bathroom so that she had to step back.

He shut the door behind them. "Talk. Now." His expression was so full of concern that she wanted to cry.

"Look, it's—"

"Don't say nothing. Please tell me what's going on, Grace."

Oh, she didn't want to do this here, but she could tell he wasn't letting this go and it was eating her up inside to keep it from him. "Fine, but for the record, I didn't want to ruin tonight."

"Are you breaking up with me?"

She blinked, shocked. "No...I realized I missed my period. So I took a pregnancy test." She might as well just get it out there. "It came back positive, but it might mean nothing. I'm going to see a doctor next week and have them do a blood test. It'll be more accurate."

He dropped his arms from his defensive stance and stared at her. "Are you serious?"

Her insides squirmed, her heart thudding in her ears. "I know we used a lot of condoms that night a month ago, but maybe one broke or something."

"That's..."

"You don't have to say anything. It's why I didn't want to bring this up here. In fact, I'm sorry I did." She closed her eyes for a long moment and took a deep breath.

"Grace, if you're pregnant, we'll get married and—"

Her eyes snapped open. "Whoa, whoa, whoa. Stop right there. No one is getting married."

"I love you." He said the words so simply.

"Logan! Seriously, stop. We're not doing this in your guest bathroom."

"Why not? I *do* love you and if you're pregnant, we *are* getting married."

The tension headache that had been teasing her fully spread across the back of her skull now. "You're not seriously telling me we're going to get married in a freaking bathroom right now. Let's just wait until I go see a doctor, okay? Then we'll make some decisions."

"Why do you keep pushing me away?"

"I'm not pushing you away! I just don't want to talk about this right now."

"I know you got burned by your ex. But I am not him. Not even close. And if I ever see that loser again—"

"Oh my God, I don't want to talk about him."

"Why not? I feel like he's always in the room with us. As if I'm being blamed for things he did!"

Her eyes widened. "You can't be serious."

"No...I didn't mean that. I don't know why I said that. I'm just frustrated. I do understand why you wanted to take things slow, but if you're pregnant—"

"We'll cross that bridge if I am. Let's wait until next week and figure things out. Until then let's just go back out there and pretend everything's...normal."

His jaw tightened. "Are you going to say anything about the fact that I told you I love you?"

"You don't mean that," she snapped. "You're just saying that because you think I might be pregnant." There was no way that he just all of a sudden had the urge to declare his feelings of love. If he had, he would have told her last night in the hotel room. It had been Christmas and would have been the perfect way to end the day. No way he'd just realized it right this instant.

"Now you're telling me how I feel?"

She stared at him, wondering how this conversation had gotten so twisted up. "No I'm not, I'm not trying to." She shoved past him and tugged the bathroom door open. "I'm not doing this now. I simply can't." It was getting difficult to breathe and she felt as if she was suffocating in that tiny room. She certainly didn't want to have an argument in front of his family, but as she stepped into the hall and came face-to-face with his mom she realized that the woman had definitely overheard at least some of their conversation.

Oh, crap. Crap, crap, crap.

His mom looked like a deer caught in headlights as she stood there. "I was just on my way..." She cleared her throat and turned around, hurrying down the hallway as Logan stepped out.

"I'm just going to go," Grace murmured, near tears again. She was emotionally done for the night, needed to get away from Logan.

"No." Gently grasping her shoulders, he turned her around. "Don't leave. We'll figure this out, but *together*."

"Honestly, I'm pretty close to having a breakdown right now. And I really don't want to cry in front of your family. Please make excuses for me and thank everybody." Without waiting for a response, she hurried to the kitchen and grabbed her purse.

Maybe this was the wrong decision, but everything felt like too much all of a sudden. The entire last week, the attacks, now thinking she might be pregnant? No. She hadn't even wanted to come tonight, had wanted time to process it herself first.

Which was what she should've done. She should have listened to her instincts.

"Grace, at least let me walk you to your car." Logan was on her heels, though definitely not trying to stop her.

She wasn't sure if that made her feel better or worse as he fell in step with her.

When she got in her car, he held his hand on the door so she couldn't open it. "You don't have to go," he rasped out, looking down at her, his expression miserable.

"This isn't about you, I promise. I'm just really stressed out. And I don't want to cry in front of your parents." She was already embarrassed enough about leaving right now. She felt like an emotional wreck and could only imagine how crazy they would think she was.

"Trust me, they'll understand. But I don't want you to leave." There was so much longing in his expression, but she knew that if she stayed, things would just get worse.

She couldn't paste on a fake smile tonight, and he wasn't going to let this go. "I'll text you when I get home."

Jaw tight, he stepped back, his expression unreadable as she got into the driver's seat.

She hated leaving but right now she knew it was the best thing to do. For both of them.

As she pulled out of the driveway, she forced herself not to look back at Logan. She felt like a big pile of crap right now, and looking at him was only going to make it worse. She wasn't sure what had happened, but everything had gone wrong, had gotten so damn twisted so quickly.

She probably shouldn't have reacted the way she had, but him telling her that he loved her and wanted to marry her in a tiny bathroom directly after she'd told him she might be pregnant had felt so fake and forced. She knew he cared for her, but love and marriage were a big step.

When she got married or if they ever got to the point where they admitted they loved each other, she wanted it to mean something. And she didn't want it to be because of obligation.

She wanted it to be real, to be his number one priority. Not something he said out of pity or charity.

As she turned out of his neighborhood, her phone rang. For an instant her heart leapt when she thought it was him calling her. Yes, she'd told him she needed space, but she was still human.

When she saw Sierra's number on the screen instead, she contemplated not answering only because of where her headspace was. But she missed talking to her friend. She pressed the call system on her car. "Hey, what's up?"

"Hey yourself. I heard you guys are home free. I miss you and wanted to see when we can get together."

"Oh, I don't know, anytime is great." For some reason her voice cracked.

"What's wrong?"

"Nothing. Everything." She ordered herself to stop crying but it was too late. And Sierra was one of her best friends. If she couldn't be vulnerable with her friends, then what was the point?

"Where are you right now?"

"I'm headed home."

"Well Hayden got called into work last minute. Some security issue. He's going to be there all night and probably most of tomorrow. You want to come over and have a girls' night?"

"This feels a little made up and a lot like pity."

Sierra snorted. "I'm not making it up. He really is gone. And it's definitely not pity. We have so many leftover desserts from Christmas. Come save me from myself."

"Come save you from all the desserts you baked?" she asked laughingly even as she turned back in the direction of Sierra's house. The thought of going home was too depressing.

"Absolutely. I'm completely out of control. So that's a yes?"

"Yes. I'm headed that way already. I'll be there in ten minutes."

As they disconnected, she felt a little bit better. But not much. Grace felt lost and there were too many things out of her control right now. Like the fact that she might be having a baby.

For now at least, she was going to drown herself in desserts and sugar and try not to obsess over the argument she and Logan had just had.

CHAPTER 30

"Are you moping out here?" Taylor plopped down in the seat next to Logan as he stared out at his pool.

He had a beer on the table next to him that he hadn't touched in the last twenty minutes so it was likely lukewarm by now. He didn't care. "Just relaxing." That was a lie, but what else was he going to say? That he was feeling sorry for himself? Grace had texted him a while ago to let him know she was at Sierra's and would be staying there for the night.

Even though the threat was gone, it still made him feel better to know she wasn't alone tonight. He just wished that they were together, that he was in her bed. Or she was in his. No, he wished they'd never gotten into an argument at all.

"Talk to me, goose."

He snorted and looked over at his sister-in-law, a woman who'd been a godsend for his serious brother. "You're feeling chatty tonight."

"It's all the eggnog. It's gone to my head. Come on, what's going on? I know you and Grace had a fight or something. No way she would have left like that otherwise."

"Or something." His mom hadn't said a word about it to anyone and he'd made an excuse about Grace having to hurry off.

"Come on," Taylor continued. "I also got a text from Sierra telling me Grace is over there and crying."

"She's crying?" Now he felt like shit. Well, even more so.

"I doubt you made her cry. So what's up?"

"I know I can trust you with anything," he said. It was true; his sister-in-law was like a vault. His brother had gotten incredibly lucky finding her. And the two complemented each other in a way Logan had never thought he would have for himself. Until he'd met Grace. "But I'm going to preface this by saying we are in a trust circle right now."

She giggled slightly. "A trust circle? Seriously?"

"Grace uses the phrase at work." She'd used it once with him, then explained how she used it with the kids at school. Nothing left the trust circle.

"I know, I'm just messing with you. So what's up?"

He filled her in on the brief version of everything that had transpired in the bathroom. He also ignored her little winces as he talked. "So what's the verdict?" he asked once he'd finished.

"Look, there's no bad guy right now. You guys had your first official argument. You're just getting to a different and new place in your relationship. And telling a woman that you love her and want to marry her because she thinks she's pregnant? I mean, I get the thought process behind it because I know you, but...a bathroom probably wasn't the best place to drop all that on her. She's very likely trying to process that she might be pregnant. Not to mention you guys just went through a whole lot with that guy literally trying to kill you. Multiple times. And it *just* happened."

He turned away and looked back out at the pool. "I know. I know it in my head. I just... I meant everything I said." He looked over at Taylor to see her reaction. Because yeah, he loved Grace. And she hadn't believed him. That struck deep.

Taylor didn't look surprised at all as she took a sip of her eggnog. "I know," she said, setting the glass on the table between them. "I've also known Grace a long time. Her ex really messed with her self-esteem. And I know you don't know her and her mom together, but let me tell you her mom is a piece of work too. Grace will never say the words, but it's like she doesn't feel worthy of being loved. I guarantee she didn't believe you when you told her that you love her."

He scrubbed a hand over his face. He'd gotten that feeling too. "So should I call her?"

"Yeah, but not tonight. She needs to process this in her own time and she's probably asleep now anyway."

He scowled. "That's not very helpful at all."

"Please, I am a wealth of wisdom."

Despite his dark mood he found himself laughing lightly. "Is that what you tell Roman?"

"Every single day I remind him how awesome I am." Grinning, she took a sip of her eggnog and leaned back.

He shook his head even as that knot twisted in his gut. Damn, he missed Grace already. But Taylor was right—he wasn't going to call her tonight. He would text her though, tell her he was thinking about her.

And the next time he saw her, he was going to make it clear that he did love her. He was pretty sure he'd already shown her, she just needed to believe it. And baby or not, he loved her and wasn't walking away. That wasn't changing. He loved everything about her. As far as a baby? He wasn't sure how he felt. And yeah, he figured that was ironic. Grace didn't know how she felt either so of course she would need time to wrap her head around it.

Though he wanted to call her, to push to see her, he held off. He could give her a little space. For now.

CHAPTER 31

She wasn't pregnant!

Grace wanted to shout it from the rooftops. Or at least from her front porch. She'd texted Logan minutes ago as she left her OB's office telling him she wanted to talk to him in person whenever he was free.

They hadn't talked since their belated Christmas party, which, granted, was only two and a half days ago, but it was Monday afternoon and she missed him. And she felt bad for the way she'd reacted.

She'd kept expecting him to call but maybe he'd had to work. She thought Mr. Christiansen had let him off for a while but maybe he'd been called in. Or *maybe* he was giving her the space she'd asked for. *Ugh.* Now she wished she'd never asked for it.

Either way, the relief pulsing through her right now was incredible. She wasn't ready to think about having a baby and all that entailed. She and Logan had literally just started a relationship.

Or maybe they didn't even have one anymore. She hadn't left things on great terms, so who knew at this point? He'd told her he loved her and she'd practically thrown it in his face, unwilling to believe him. At that thought, her brief moment of joy was doused.

But when she turned into her driveway and saw Logan's borrowed truck there, surprise jumped inside her.

She was so happy to see him. *Always.* And she was always thinking about him. No matter what, it was like he was hanging out in the back of her mind, this wonderful man she didn't know what she'd done to deserve. She just hoped she hadn't pushed him away with her fear.

She quickly threw her car into park and jumped out.

He stepped out of the truck in jeans and a black sweater, looking good enough to eat as usual. He clearly hadn't shaved since Friday and had some serious scruff that somehow made him look even sexier. He wasn't smiling, but he didn't look angry either. That had to be a good thing.

"I'm not pregnant," she blurted as he shut his door behind him. "I wanted to tell you in person."

He looked mildly surprised as he approached her. "Okay."

"Okay?"

"I don't know how I feel about that. Honestly, I wouldn't have been sad if you had been. And I figure this is the kind of thing I need to be honest about. I'm not ready for kids right now but if you'd been pregnant, then we would have made it work."

Now it was her turn to blink in surprise. "I'm not ready for kids, just FYI. I want them eventually, but for now it's too soon for me."

He stood a foot in front of her, looking nervous, and she hated that.

"I'm sorry," she blurted at the same time he said the exact same thing.

Just like that, it was as if the tension eased out of both of them.

"Look, I really am sorry about Friday," she continued. "And I feel like a lunatic for leaving like that. I was just having a really hard time processing everything, and it turns out I didn't really handle the whole attempted murder thing too well." She hadn't been sleeping at all because of it. She'd wanted to reach out to him, but had been too afraid of rejection.

His expression softened slightly and he stepped closer, gently putting one of his big hands on her hip in a possessive way she melted at. Okay, so maybe she hadn't screwed things up between them.

"I kind of figured it was going to take a while for you to adjust to everything. Did you have nightmares?"

She nodded. "I kept dreaming that we were running, but this time the monster caught up with us." She shuddered at the remnants of the nightmares still lingering inside her. "I know time will make it better but it sucks right now. I don't know how you dealt with... Well, all you've dealt with." Because she wasn't sure what he'd gone through overseas. Not exactly.

"Therapy," he said, all serious. "I talked to someone for about a year after I got home. And before we go any further I need to say something. I'm sorry I basically told you that we were getting married instead of actually asking. When I've thought about proposing to you—"

"What?"

He didn't smile as she expected him to. Instead his expression remained serious, his dark eyes pinned to hers. "Yes, I've thought about proposing. Not in the near future, but this is serious for me. Apparently I haven't been as forthcoming as I should have been. I thought giving you time to adjust to us dating was the smart thing to do, considering the way things ended with your asshole ex. But I'm serious about you, Grace. I see a future with you. And I love you. I didn't just say that because you thought you might be pregnant. I do *love* you. I've known that for months."

She stared up at him in shock, her heart expanding. "I—"

He gently flexed his hand on her hip, his expression softening just a bit. "You don't have to say it just because I did."

"I know. But I do love you. I've been denying it even to myself for a while. I feel like a mess sometimes, like I'm never going to get that happy ending other people get. But I love you so much, Logan." It felt liberating to say the words.

He cupped her cheek with one hand. "Why don't you think you deserve a happy ending?"

"I don't know," she whispered, wrapping her arms around him. "I know I deserve it just as much as anyone else. I guess I'm just afraid it's not going to happen for me."

"Well I'm not walking away from you, Grace. If you're not serious about me, you need to tell me right now."

She tightened her grip around him. "I just said that I love you."

His lips kicked up, the mischievous Logan she knew well in full view. "I know. I just wanted to hear you say it again."

All the tension inside her eased. "Was this our first argument?"

"I think so. But I also think making up will be—"

Suddenly he turned, shoving her behind him.

She stumbled in her sneakers, falling against the side of his truck. "What the—"

Her breath caught in her throat when she saw a fit-looking man in his thirties wearing jeans and a dark hoodie pulled up over his head, holding a gun low at his side, pointed right at them.

"Start walking to the house," he said quietly.

Grace's throat tightened with pure panic. Across the street her neighbor was unloading groceries, and two doors down she could hear another neighbor's kids playing in the front yard. Dear God, what was going on? Who was this guy?

Logan shoved her behind him.

"Hands where I can see them," the man snapped out.

"You don't want to do this." Logan kept his hands slightly out, palms up so the guy could see them.

Grace was frozen in place, half behind Logan, unable to move as she stared at the gun. Her phone was still in her car and so was her pepper spray. Not that pepper spray was going to do a hell of a lot of good at this distance against a man with a gun.

"Don't tell me what I need to do. You ruined my parents' marriage. You destroyed my dad." His voice was quiet, but rage filled every word, his expression dark.

Oh God, no. This had to be Austin Brister's son.

"Why don't you put the gun down and walk away? You won't get away with this." Logan's voice was calm while Grace's heart raced out of control, a fast, erratic beat.

"You have no idea what I'll get away with," the man snarled. He took a menacing step forward. "I'm not going to tell you twice. Get in the house."

Grace peered around Logan and somehow found her voice. "My keys are still in the car," she whispered. She didn't want to go into her house but she also didn't want to be shot in her front yard. Maybe if the guy was distracted, they could...

No, he kept his weapon trained on them as he retrieved her keys, and her neighbors didn't notice anything strange going on. They were so involved in their day-to-day lives, which was normal. Because people didn't expect random gunmen to show up and hold their neighbors hostage.

The man tossed the keys to Logan, who caught them in one hand, his reflexes lightning quick.

"You open the door," he said to Logan. "And then you come back here with me."

Logan kept his hands out so Grace could move around him. "Look, she's not part of this, just let her go—" He stopped as the man took another menacing step forward, his face tightening.

"Inside now or I'll shoot you both right here. Then who knows, maybe those kids across the street might get hit too."

Grace took the decision out of Logan's hands and stepped around him.

"Open the door." She understood that this shooter wanted Logan in front and she was supposed to remain behind him as a sort of buffer, ensuring Logan wouldn't attack the guy.

It was smart and terrible.

But if they could just get him away from her neighbors, away from innocent kids and into an enclosed space, maybe Logan could take the guy out. She knew he had the training, and at this point, this was the only chance they had. They just had to take the upper hand.

Somehow.

Feeling numb, mind racing, she stepped toward the man as Logan walked up the little steps of her cottage-style house. As Logan opened the front door, her security alarm started beeping.

"Disarm it." The man shoved her slightly and she stumbled forward through the door.

Heart racing, she moved around Logan and started to plug in the emergency code—the one that would actually silence it but still send out a distress call. But Logan must have seen an opening.

Out of the corner of her eye she saw him lunge at the other man. She fell against the wall as the two men rammed into her. The gun fell, clattering to the floor.

Her head slammed against the security pad of the alarm under the impact of their bodies. As the alarm kept beeping, she rolled out of the way, watching Logan slam his fist into the guy's gut.

But the other man was clearly fit and got a shot in, punching Logan in the face.

Grace scrambled to her hands and knees, heart racing. The gun! She had to get to the gun.

CHAPTER 32

Logan was in a fight for his life. For Grace's life.

He had to stop this guy. He'd seen the file on Brister's family and this was his oldest son, Steven—who was supposed to be working in London right now.

Not that it mattered. The only thing that mattered was getting him down and keeping him down.

Logan dodged another blow to the face, coming up with a left uppercut to Steven's jaw as the alarm started full-on blaring.

Brister's head snapped back but he barely stumbled. Instead he went into a bull stance and ran at Logan, clipping him right in the middle.

Logan took the impact and rolled back onto the floor. As he did, he jabbed the guy hard with three quick punches right to the kidney. He needed to find the dropped pistol, but couldn't pause long enough to look where it had fallen.

As they tumbled to the ground, Brister groaned in raw agony at the blows. He rolled onto his side, trying to get away from Logan.

Logan, still on the floor too, kicked out, slamming his boot into Brister's stomach before jumping to his feet. This guy was staying down.

"Freeze! Don't you dare move!" Grace shouted above the now blaring alarm.

Logan looked over at her, her hands trembling as she held a pistol on Brister, who was struggling to his feet.

Logan didn't waste any time, simply strode over to her and plucked the weapon from her hands, never taking his eyes off Brister. He trained the weapon on him. "Stay on the ground and get on your stomach," he snapped. Then he said to Grace, "I've got some zip ties in my truck. Back seat in a duffel bag. Go grab them. Call the police." They'd probably already been alerted because of the alarm but he wanted her to call them anyway.

Moments later she was back with the zip ties, eyes a little dilated with shock.

"Go back outside while I tie him up," he said as he took the ties from her. He wanted her as far away from this madness as possible. Brister was on the ground, staring at him with murder in his eyes, but he was remaining still.

"Should I turn off the alarm?"

"Yes, now go." He kept the weapon pinned on Brister as she disarmed it. In the following silence Logan strode toward his prisoner. "Move and you'll make my decision to end you really easy," he growled.

Brister snarled in anger, but didn't try to fight him as Logan quickly secured his hands behind his back. For good measure, he secured his ankles together as well. This guy wasn't going anywhere. And Logan wasn't moving from his side until the cops showed up.

Thankfully sirens wailed in the distance, growing closer and closer.

And Grace was safe. The woman he loved was okay.

Until that moment, he thought he knew fear. Because he'd been afraid before overseas. Would have been stupid not to have a healthy dose of fear. And then in the desert with Grace he'd been worried.

This... *Hell.* Grace had come so close to being shot. Killed.

He was going to be having nightmares about today for a while.

CHAPTER 33

"I'm ready to go home." Grace hoped she didn't sound like she was whining. She was just exhausted, that being the understatement of the century. She was done with people trying to kill her and Logan.

Logan, who'd taken her hand in his a while ago, simply squeezed her fingers. "We'll get out of here soon enough."

Here being Hurley's office, where they were currently holed up and waiting for the detective to return. The man had been in and out for the last couple hours even after they'd given their statements.

"You don't think they're going to let him go or anything, do you?"

Logan snorted. "No way. I think Hurley just wants to keep us updated with what's going on. He's dealing with a lot of shit right now."

Almost on cue, the detective stepped into his office and shut the door, his expression unreadable as he moved around his desk. But when he sat down with a sigh, he gave them a half-smile. "Thank you both for being patient. I wanted to tie up a few things before I let you go. I'm tired of seeing you guys in here, for your sakes. We still have a lot of things to figure out at this point, but Steven Brister got into the country using a private plane. Apparently that's why his dad was down here in Vegas. He didn't leave Montana to come after you. He came down here to stop his son."

Logan straightened slightly in his seat. "How did he even know his son was here?"

"He told his dad what he was going to do in a roundabout way. Brister—senior—tried to stop him but his son told him he was going to 'take care of things.' I guess Steven had stopped in to see his mom after arriving from London. He thought she was overreacting to the abuse and tried to convince her to give his dad a second chance. I'm sure there are more details we'll never be privy to but I talked to their daughter, Steven's sister. She told him to leave their mom alone until he could get his head out of his ass. Apparently he didn't take that well and decided to pay Logan a visit. Steven is in finance but he was in the army for four years, so he's got a decent amount of training. And he definitely has the technical knowledge to have tracked your phone. Or hired someone to do it. We're still figuring out all the details, but we've now got his laptop in custody and our tech guys are digging through it. All the bread crumbs are going to lead back to him. I'm sure of it."

"You really don't think his dad was involved?"

He shook his head. "No. I really don't. He's old-school, and the timeline doesn't fit anyway. That was the thing that bothered me before. I mean *technically* he could've gotten here to attack you that first time, but there was just too small of a window from when he left and getting here. He's back in Montana now in custody without bail. I don't know what's gonna happen to him and I don't actually care. His son is under arrest for attempted murder. If it goes to trial, you guys will need to testify. That's something else I wanted to talk to you about before I cut you loose."

"We'll testify," Grace said, even as Logan murmured the same.

"I didn't doubt that, but I still wanted to let you know it might be a possibility. He's not getting off easy for this. He came after you on multiple occasions, stalking you, holding you at gunpoint—there are a whole list of crimes he's going away for. And the prosecutor wants to take him down *hard* since this was so premeditated."

Grace simply nodded, finally feeling relief for the first time about the whole mess. They could go home, return to their lives. "Thank you."

"Don't thank me. I...I wish we'd caught him earlier. We pushed Austin Brister hard. But I should've seen this."

"How could you have seen this coming?" Logan asked as he stood, tugging Grace with him.

She stood, grabbing her purse. "You guys found Austin Brister at a motel in Vegas after he cut his tracking anklet. Of course you assumed he was behind this," Grace added. "We did too. We're grateful the right person is locked up now. And we're going home. *Now*. Unless you desperately need us for something, please don't call," she said gently. She wanted to sleep for twenty-four hours and not think about any of this, just lose herself in Logan.

The detective gave her a real smile and rounded the desk to shake both their hands. "I hope you guys get some rest. And you're free to return to your home. It's not a crime scene."

"My place or yours?" Logan asked once they were out in the hallway. He tucked her tight against him, his big, warm body comforting.

They could have died today, might never have had the chance at their happily ever after she now realized she deserved. "Either one is fine with me. As long as we go together." She just wanted to be with Logan.

"Let's go to mine this time. And...I think we should move in with each other soon."

She looked up at him in surprise. "Yeah?"

"Yeah. I'm going to be in your bed every night no matter what. So let's make it official. I don't care which house either. We'll rent out the other one."

"Okay."

He nearly stumbled in surprise as they reached the exit. "That's it?"

"That's it. Because I love you." She'd been resisting Logan for too long. And she was done with that, done not going for what she wanted. Logan had shown her exactly who he was—a wonderful, honorable man—and that he loved her. She was going to hold on to him tight.

EPILOGUE

Logan stepped out onto his patio, smiling to see Grace stretched out on the lounge chair looking perfectly sexy and content. In jeans and a sweater, she was reading a book and was definitely in her happy place tonight.

A month and a half had passed since Steven Brister had tried to kill them and they were finally back to normal. Brister had agreed to plea to slightly lesser charges instead of going through with a trial. Either way he was going to be in jail for a long time. And according to Wyatt, Heidi Brister had almost finalized the divorce. Supposedly Austin Brister was torn up about his son and was showing remorse for years of abuse against his wife but Logan didn't buy it. The guy could live with his guilt. Brister senior was going to jail too, but it was a slap on the wrist compared to his son.

All that was behind Logan and Grace now. He didn't want to think about any of that ever again. He just wanted to live his life with the woman he loved.

"Are you going to pass out on me right there?" he asked, champagne bottle in hand. He certainly hoped not, because he had plans for her.

Laughing, she set her book down. "Maybe. I think that's the best dinner you've ever cooked."

"Well, it's Valentine's Day. I wanted it to be special."

"Every day with you is special." Standing, she crossed over to him and he drank in every inch of her.

Yeah, he felt the exact same way. Which is why he was feeling nervous as hell about tonight. He'd cooked a huge spread of surf and turf for her and they'd just been lounging in front of the pool since then, talking and making out like teenagers until he'd started to clear all the dishes. She'd tried to help but he'd wanted her to relax while he got his head on straight.

Soon enough he was going to take her back inside and make love to her until they both passed out. But he desperately needed to do something else first.

"You feel like some champagne?" Damn, did he sound weird?

"You don't need to ask twice." Despite the chill in the air, she had on a sexy red wraparound sweater that cut low, showing off all sorts of cleavage he wanted to bury his face against.

Before popping the cork, he dipped his head down and brushed his mouth over hers even as he gently cupped one of her breasts through her sweater. He loved being able to touch her, kiss her, anytime he wanted. And he really loved when she initiated things. They'd been living together a month and a half, and about half of those mornings he woke up with her naked and on top of him.

Very soon he hoped to be naked again.

He'd gone back and forth all day, questioning himself on whether this was too soon, but he knew in his heart that Grace was it for him. And the last month and a half had been incredible. He felt like he'd been waiting for her his entire life.

She plucked the champagne bottle from his hand. "I'll open this. Last time you almost took out a window with the cork."

After she popped it open, he took over and started pouring glasses for them, then held one out to her. "To us."

She clinked glasses with him, a soft, happy smile on her face. God, he loved her. "To us."

Before he could second-guess himself, he went down on one knee.

She blinked at him, her dark hair tumbling around her face. Staring, she set her glass on the table as he pulled out a jewelry box. He popped it open but before he could say another word, she shouted, "Yes!"

Just like that, all the stupid tension inside him drained away. He fought back a laugh. "I want it official. Yes, you will marry me?"

She cupped his cheeks with her soft hands and bent her head to kiss him all over as she laughed. "Yes, yes, yes."

More than satisfied, he slid the ring on her finger as he stood, then scooped her up into his arms. She let out a little yelp as he said, "Upstairs, or out here?"

"Upstairs for sure. I don't want to give our neighbors a show."

Grinning, he kissed her mouth hard as he hurried back inside. Hell, who cared about champagne? He had his future wife in his arms and she was everything.

He was going to spend the next couple hours bringing her all the pleasure she deserved, marking the start of the rest of their lives together.

Dear Readers

I hope you enjoyed Logan's story! If you'd like to stay in touch and be the first to learn about new releases you can:

Check out my website for book news: https://www.katiereus.com

Also, please consider leaving a review at one of your favorite online retailers. It's a great way to help other readers discover new books and I appreciate all reviews.

Happy reading,
Katie

ABOUT THE AUTHOR

Katie Reus is the *USA Today* bestselling author of the Red Stone Security series, the Ancients Rising series and the Redemption Harbor series. She fell in love with romance at a young age thanks to books she pilfered from her mom's stash. Years later she loves reading romance almost as much as she loves writing it.

However, she didn't always know she wanted to be a writer. After changing majors many times, she finally graduated summa cum laude with a degree in psychology. Not long after that she discovered a new love. Writing. She now spends her days writing paranormal romance and sexy romantic suspense.

COMPLETE BOOKLIST

Ancients Rising
Ancient Protector
Ancient Enemy
Ancient Enforcer
Ancient Vendetta
Ancient Retribution
Ancient Vengeance
Ancient Sentinel
Ancient Warrior
Ancient Guardian

Darkness Series
Darkness Awakened
Taste of Darkness
Beyond the Darkness
Hunted by Darkness
Into the Darkness
Saved by Darkness
Guardian of Darkness
Sentinel of Darkness

A Very Dragon Christmas

Darkness Rising

Deadly Ops Series

Targeted

Bound to Danger

Chasing Danger

Shattered Duty

Edge of Danger

A Covert Affair

Endgame Trilogy

Bishop's Knight

Bishop's Queen

Bishop's Endgame

Holiday With a Hitman Series

How the Hitman Stole Christmas

A Very Merry Hitman

MacArthur Family Series

Falling for Irish

Unintended Target

Saving Sienna

Moon Shifter Series

Alpha Instinct

Lover's Instinct

Primal Possession

Mating Instinct

His Untamed Desire

Avenger's Heat
Hunter Reborn
Protective Instinct
Dark Protector
A Mate for Christmas

O'Connor Family Series
Merry Christmas, Baby
Tease Me, Baby
It's Me Again, Baby
Mistletoe Me, Baby

Red Stone Security Series®
No One to Trust
Danger Next Door
Fatal Deception
Miami, Mistletoe & Murder
His to Protect
Breaking Her Rules
Protecting His Witness
Sinful Seduction
Under His Protection
Deadly Fallout
Sworn to Protect
Secret Obsession
Love Thy Enemy
Dangerous Protector
Lethal Game
Secret Enemy
Saving Danger
Guarding Her

Deadly Protector
Danger Rising
Protecting Rebel

Redemption Harbor® Series
Resurrection
Savage Rising
Dangerous Witness
Innocent Target
Hunting Danger
Covert Games
Chasing Vengeance

Redemption Harbor® Security
Fighting for Hailey
Fighting for Reese
Fighting for Adalyn
Fighting for Magnolia

Sin City Series (the Serafina)
First Surrender
Sensual Surrender
Sweetest Surrender
Dangerous Surrender
Deadly Surrender

Verona Bay Series
Dark Memento
Deadly Past
Silent Protector

www.ingramcontent.com/pod-product-compliance
Lightning Source LLC
Chambersburg PA
CBHW030430120726
47903CB00003B/899